CHRISTMAS TRESS AND MISTLETOE

The idea of another family Christmas fills Fran with dread, particularly when she is asked to pick up her mother's latest charity case and bring him along. But Ryan Conway is not what she was expecting. He is looking after his young niece while his sister is in hospital, and Fran decides the pair of them may not be such bad company after all. Then, once the festivities are in full swing, Santa arrives unexpectedly — and Fran's life changes forever . . .

FAY CUNNINGHAM

CHRISTMAS TREES AND MISTLETOE

Complete and Unabridged

LINFORD
Leicester

First published in Great Britain in 2016

First Linford Edition
published 2017

A catalogue record for this book is available
from the British Library.

ISBN 978–1–4448–3471–0

Published by
F. A. Thorpe (Publishing)
Anstey, Leicestershire

Set by Words & Graphics Ltd.
Anstey, Leicestershire
Printed and bound in Great Britain by
T. J. International Ltd., Padstow, Cornwall

This book is printed on acid-free paper

1

Fran unlocked the door to her small apartment and threw the bags she had been carrying on to the sofa.

She hated Christmas shopping. Really, really hated it. How anyone could possibly enjoy it totally eluded her. It was the day before Christmas Eve and she had just spent two hours being almost crushed to death in various department stores. Her feet had swollen to twice their normal size, her arms ached from carrying heavy bags of shopping, and she still hadn't found a present for her mother. Everything was far too expensive for her meagre budget, and whatever she bought her mother would almost certainly be met by a puzzled look or a raised eyebrow. The darned woman already had everything she needed.

Maybe that was the answer, Fran thought as she kicked off her shoes

— buy her mother something she didn't need.

Pleased with the idea, Fran shrugged out of her coat and poured herself a glass of wine. She had definitely earned it. In a little while she would look on the internet for something totally unnecessary for her mother, but right this minute all she wanted to do was sit and relax. She had turned the heating up before she went out and the room was warm and comfortable. With a sigh of contentment, she put her feet up on the coffee table and rested her head against one of the many cushions littering her sofa.

The ringing of the telephone brought her sharply out of a pleasant doze. Cursing quietly to herself, she reached for the mobile phone jigging around on the table in front of her.

'Francesca? Is that you?'

Who else would it be? Fran almost cancelled the call. She knew her mother was going to ask her to do something she didn't want to do, and she had already done quite enough for one day.

'Yes, Mother, of course it's me. I live here.'

'You are still coming tomorrow, aren't you?'

'I always come to you for Christmas, and I'll be there as usual this year. I already told you that.'

'I know you did, dear, but I have a favour to ask.'

Here it comes, Fran thought. She was about to protest, but her mother didn't give her a chance.

'An old friend of mine has a daughter about your age, and the daughter has just had an emergency operation. She'll be spending Christmas in hospital.'

Fran held the phone away from her ear and frowned at it. What did her mother's friend's daughter have to do with her? She put the phone back to her ear when she realised her mother was still talking.

'The daughter is a widow,' Vanessa Sutherland continued. 'Her husband died two years ago. She has a little girl, and her brother will have to look after the child over Christmas. I suggested the brother and his niece spend the Christmas holiday with us.'

Fran heaved out a sigh. Another lame duck for Christmas. Last year it had been a homeless person her mother had picked up in the town centre on Christmas Eve.

'You can invite whoever you like, Mother,' she said carefully. She had a feeling she was about to get involved in her mother's benevolence yet again.

'I know that, Francesca, but the brother lives right near you so I'd like you to pick him up tomorrow and bring him down here.'

'Doesn't he have a car of his own?' Asking questions was a way of gaining some time. Vanessa had a habit of railroading people into doing what she wanted before they had a chance to think it through.

'Most probably,' her mother said impatiently. 'I think he works in a garage. But it would be silly to bring two cars.' When Fran didn't answer, her voice took on a wheedling tone. 'Please, Francesca. I'm sure he's a very nice man, and it won't take you out of your way.'

'You've already told him I'll pick him up, haven't you?' Fran let out an audible sigh. 'OK. Where does he live?'

The man's address was several miles away, but she made a note of his telephone number and promised to call him later. She was tired and hungry and needed some food inside her before she did anything. She ended the call and lay back on the sofa with her eyes closed.

Two minutes later the phone rang again. 'Hello,' she said rather curtly. She couldn't cope with another of her mother's thinly veiled demands.

The voice on the other end of the phone didn't belong to her mother. It was deep and sexy and quite definitely male. 'Hi, I'm Ryan Conway. I'm really sorry to bother you, but I believe our mothers know one another. My mother lives in Spain, and she phoned to tell me I'll be spending Christmas with you. I just wanted to let you know I really appreciate your mother's kind invitation, but I already have everything organized.'

Fran liked the sound of his voice, but she thought it was a bit uncharitable to turn down her mother's invitation quite so bluntly. 'So you've already made up your mind you don't want to spend Christmas with me. Considering you've never even met me, I find that quite rude.'

She listened to his floundering apology for a few seconds before she took pity on him. 'I'm sorry,' she said. 'To be honest, I don't want to go out of my way to pick you up tomorrow, either, but it seems we've both been bulldozed into this by our mothers. My name is Fran Sutherland, and I have a flat in Willesden Green. My mother lives near Hazelmere in Surrey, and I promised I'd be there in time for lunch tomorrow, so we need to leave at about ten thirty to allow for traffic.'

The silence on the other end of the phone lasted for such a long time that Fran began to feel sorry for the poor man. They had both been blindsided by their mothers, and now she was adding to his discomfort. 'You don't have to come,' she told him. 'I can tell my mother you have other plans.'

'You could do that,' he said. 'But then what do I tell *my* mother?'

Fran sighed. 'Then I guess we're stuck with one another. Be ready by ten thirty tomorrow morning. I already have your address.'

She hung up before he could answer. Damn the man. He didn't sound the slightest bit grateful, just annoyed because he had been coerced into doing something he didn't want to do. Well, unfortunately that happened to everyone.

She still had things to do before she left in the morning, and she had to pack her suitcase. She looked in her wardrobe and decided the copper-coloured cashmere dress she had bought a couple of weeks ago, purely on impulse, might be worth popping in her case. When she tried it on it skimmed her hips and clung where necessary, the colour accenting her russet hair and amber eyes perfectly. She usually wore jeans at Christmas because she couldn't see the point of dressing up. She had to look smart for work every day of the week, and this was supposed to be a holiday. Fran had been told what to wear when she was a child and she refused to do it anymore.

By the time she had sorted out heels to go with the dress and folded her prettiest pyjamas, she was beginning to feel a bit ridiculous. She took the dress out of the case and hung it back in the wardrobe, swapping the pyjamas for a warm nightgown. She usually slept in her birthday suit, even in the winter, but she knew the old house could feel cold, and there was always the chance of meeting someone on the stairs.

She looked at herself in her bedroom

mirror. What on earth was she doing, getting all silly over the sound of a voice on the phone? She knew all too well how deceptive a sexy voice could be. What had he said his name was? Ryan Conway? And he worked in a garage? Garage mechanics were obviously coming up in the world, name-wise. The nice young man who had fixed her tyre recently had been called Billy Jones.

★ ★ ★

The next morning Fran woke to the sound of rain pounding on the window and the radio announcer telling her the weather was average for this time of the year. No snow; just cold, wet and miserable. She spent a few moments enjoying the warmth of her bed before she remembered what day it was and where she had to be. Damn! She had to collect some strange man from an address on the other side of the river and then drive all the way to her mother's house in Surrey.

For some reason the radiator in her bathroom had decided not to work, and kicking it just hurt her toes. Although the water in the shower was hot, the bathroom was freezing cold, and this did nothing to improve her mood. She dressed quickly in jeans and a thick sweater and popped some toast in the toaster. Because of the detour to pickup her mother's latest charity case, she had to leave earlier than she normally would, which meant rushing her breakfast and driving further than necessary. Not a good way to start Christmas Eve.

The rain was cold and nasty and mixed with sleet. It stuck to the windscreen of her car and the wipers pushed it into a mucky heap that restricted her view. By the time she reached her destination, a row of town houses with nowhere to park, she felt thoroughly miserable. Getting out, she rang the bell and stood in the rain until the door was opened by a small child.

Fran had completely forgotten about the little girl. This was the niece who was supposed to be going with them. The child, who looked about four or five years old, had long fair hair that curled into ringlets at the tips, big blue eyes with an angry glint, and a frown that was positively scary.

Fran didn't exactly dislike children, but she didn't seek them out, either. In their place, which was as far away from her as she could manage, they were fine; but the thought of an hour's drive with a bored child didn't appeal to her in the slightest. In fact her morning had just got a hundred times worse.

'Hello,' she said tentatively. 'I've come to collect you and your uncle.' Now she sounded like a taxi driver instead of the put-upon daughter of a bossy mother.

'I don't want to go with you,' the child said. She looked Fran up and down, her mouth forming into a pout that pushed out her bottom lip. 'My mummy is in hospital and I want to stay with her.'

There were tears in the big blue eyes

now, and Fran had no idea what to do. She was just thinking about getting back in her car and driving away when a man appeared at the top of the stairs looking slightly harassed. He was tall, with dark hair he had obviously just run a hand through, and didn't look a bit like a garage mechanic. But, to be fair, she had only met garage mechanics in their place of work, usually in greasy overalls and with a spanner in their hand. She couldn't imagine this man crawling about under a car. With his athletic build and tanned face he looked more like an intrepid explorer than a mechanic, but Fran knew from experience not to generalise when it came to people. Like her grandmother was always telling her, there is more to most people than meets the eye.

'Hi, I'm Ryan — and you must be Fran.' He looked down at his niece. 'Go upstairs and get your coat, Molly.'

The child turned and started back up the stairs. She got halfway and then turned round. 'I'm not going with her.'

'Can I come inside?' Fran asked. There was no cover over the doorway and she was getting wetter by the minute. 'If there's a problem with your niece, we can deal with it in the dry.'

Ryan Conway ran a hand through his hair again, making it stand on end. 'I'm so sorry. I've never had to look after Molly on my own before, and it's not as easy as I thought it was going to be. She's just as awkward as her mother used to be when we were kids.' He waved a hand at the stairs. 'Please come up.

When she hesitated, he managed a lopsided grin. 'This is my sister's house and the living room is upstairs. I'm not trying to lure you into my bedroom or anything.'

Fran smiled politely in return, but the idea had distinct possibilities, she thought as she followed him up to the second floor. He ushered Fran into a comfortable reception room with big windows overlooking an area of parkland at the back of the house. The river glinted in the distance, and Fran could see the advantage of having the living area upstairs. The views were spectacular, and the house was only a Tube ride away from the centre of the city.

'This is lovely,' she said. Ryan's sister might be a young widow, but she had obviously been well provided for. Fran glanced around the room, noting the decorated Christmas tree in the corner and the tinsel hanging from the pictures on the walls. There was no sign of the child.

As if sensing her thoughts, Ryan sighed. 'She will have shut herself in her room. She misses her mum, and I can't do anything about that. Give her a couple of minutes and I'll go and talk to her.'

Fran felt nearly as sorry for Ryan as she did for Molly. She could picture the two of them having Christmas lunch at some small hotel whose only concession to Christmas was a decorated tree in the corner and a gold cracker beside each plate. So different from the

Christmas her mother would be organising, with a tree in almost every room and enough holly to stock a garden centre.

She still vividly remembered the Christmas when she herself was five years old. In the midst of all the frivolity, her father had said he was leaving them forever. That had been the most miserable Christmas of her life, and now it looked as if Molly's would be just as bad. She thought she might have some idea of what Molly was going through.

'Let me talk to her,' she said.

Ryan shrugged helplessly. 'Her room is up the next flight of stairs in the attic.'

Fran knocked on the door before she opened it. The room had sloping ceilings and a big window. Molly was sitting on a pretty bed covered in a pink flounced bedspread. She had stopped crying, but her face was pink and blotchy and still damp from tears.

'Listen,' Fran said, keeping her voice

friendly but firm. 'Christmas at my house will definitely be better than Christmas here without your mother, and she has to stay in hospital for a couple more days. We have three big Christmas trees, and my sister has two boys the same age as you, so you'll have someone to play with.' She sat down on the bed beside the little girl. 'And I bet your uncle wasn't going to cook you a Christmas dinner with turkey and trifle and everything, was he?'

Molly looked at her as if there might be some doubt about her sanity. 'Uncle Ryan can't cook a turkey. He's a man. Only ladies can cook turkeys. We were going to a hotel for our turkey and Christmas pudding. I don't like Christmas pudding but I like mince pies — and trifle,' she added as an afterthought.

Fran stood up and walked over to the window. Molly had an even better view from her bedroom window than the one from the living room. It was still raining — a nasty insistent drizzle that she knew would feel a lot worse than it

16

looked. If they were going to get to Surrey before lunch, it was time they left.

She looked at Molly. 'What do you think, then?'

'Do you really have *three* Christmas trees?'

'All with baubles and flashing lights.'

Molly stood up and took a coat from a hanger in a little wardrobe. 'OK then.'

When they walked into the living room, Ryan was holding his mobile phone and pacing the room, a worried expression on his face.

'Would you rather not come?' she said. 'I don't think Molly will be upset if you change your mind.'

Molly frowned. 'Yes, I will. I want to see your Christmas trees.'

Ryan stopped his pacing and looked at his niece. He gave Fran a nod of appreciation for changing the little girl's mind. 'No, of course we'll come. It was great of your mother to ask us, and you've gone out of your way to pick us up.'

'Then why do you look as if you're about to go to the dentist? I have to admit a visit to my mother always affects me that way, but you've never met her.'

'Sorry,' he said sheepishly. She got a glimpse of his smile again and thought she might forgive him for anything. 'But I feel really bad about asking for another favour. I phoned the hospital just now and they told me my sister has left a message asking me to pick up Molly's Christmas present. If we do, it'll take us out of our way by about half an hour and might make us late for lunch.'

They would have had plenty of time if it hadn't been for his niece, Fran thought wryly. 'No problem,' she said. 'We can spare half an hour.' She looked at Molly, who was busily pulling on her boots. 'Do you know what your present is, or is it a secret?'

'Even I don't know what it is,' Ryan said. 'My sister is sleeping off the anaesthetic, so she couldn't speak to me. The address sounds like a private house, so I have no idea.'

Fran laughed. 'This is getting quite exciting. I hope we can get whatever it is in my car.'

Molly got her coat and boots on in double-quick time while Ryan stacked the cases neatly in Fran's hatchback. Fran knew she could phone her mother if they got held up, but how long could it take to pick up a Christmas present? The drizzle was better than the earlier sleet, she thought as they all climbed into the car, and there was still time for it to change. Maybe it would snow tomorrow and make Molly's Christmas really special.

Fran was still at a loss to understand why she cared about the little girl. Her sister's boys had been cute as babies, but now they were at school they were noisy and boisterous. Typical boys, she supposed, but not something she wished for herself. Molly was a pretty little girl, but not particularly cute or charming. The child had her face screwed up in a scowl most of the time, but Fran was sure she had spent most of her own childhood looking exactly the same. She remembered her mother telling her if the wind changed she would be stuck with that unpleasant expression on her face forever. She remembered smiling at herself in the bathroom mirror and deciding her mother was probably right.

2

They found the address Ryan wanted without any trouble, but it wasn't what Fran had expected — and judging from the expression on Ryan's face, not what he had been expecting, either.

A long, low-bungalow sat in a large plot filled with mature trees and bushes. A wooden sign stuck on a post in the pretty front garden said 'Puppies for Sale'.

Fran risked a glance at Ryan and almost giggled at the look of shock on his face. No, he definitely hadn't been expecting this. 'Well, at least it should fit in the car,' she said cheerfully, 'unless it's a Great Dane.' She bit her lip to stop herself laughing and turned round to look at Molly. 'Can you read what the sign says?' Fran had heard the little girl trying to sound out the letters, but now Molly shook her head.

'No. The words are too long. But one of the words says p-u-p.' She looked at Fran with her big blue eyes open wide, not really daring to hope. 'Is this where you get a puppy?'

Ryan muttered a swear word under his breath. 'Listen, poppet, I think the best thing would be to leave your present here. We can pick it on the way back.' He looked helplessly at Fran. 'I can't descend on your mother with a five-year-old child *and* a puppy. It wouldn't be fair.'

'Poof,' Fran said dismissively. 'I told you my mother likes strays. She once took in a rescue cat with only three legs. Besides, I want to see what sort of puppy it is. It could be anything from a poodle to a wolfhound.' She turned round to grin at Molly. 'I told you your present would be exciting.'

A slightly harassed-looking woman with grey hair and kind brown eyes opened the door. She told them her name was Sheila French, and she listened patiently to Ryan's rather long drawn-out explanation as to why they were there.

'I know your sister slightly. We're friends on Facebook. That's how she found out I had the puppies for sale. I'm so glad you brought Molly with you. I have two puppies ready to go, so she can choose.'

Fran had been looking at the pictures on the hall wall. 'You sell Yorkshire terrier puppies?'

The woman shook her head. 'I don't sell puppies at all, normally. My sister left her dachshund with me while she went on holiday and my little dog took a liking to him. I didn't realise she was in season or I would have kept them apart. The puppies are crossbred, I'm afraid, but very pretty. We had six, but three of them are already sold and I decided to keep one myself.'

They followed Sheila into a conservatory built on the back of the bungalow. Half the space had been cordoned off to keep the puppies safely away from any open doors. Fran heard Molly's sharp intake of breath beside her. The little girl had been very quiet ever since they got out of the car, and now she was hanging back as if she was afraid to look at the puppies.

Fran took her hand. 'Are you OK, Molly?'

'Mummy said I couldn't have a puppy until I could look after it on my own.' She looked up at Fran with big, scared eyes. 'And I don't know how.'

Fran gave the small, cold hand a squeeze. 'Neither does your daddy, so you'll have to learn together. I'm pretty sure all a puppy needs is somewhere to sleep, lots of love, and plenty of food. That's not too hard, is it? You'll be fine.'

Molly moved forward and peeped over the barrier that kept the puppies at one end of the room. Ryan walked over to stand beside his niece and Fran joined them. Four little balls of fluff in various shades of brown and tan jumped up at the barrier excitedly, desperate to be petted. Sheila leant over and picked up two of the puppies, one in each hand.

'This one is already promised to someone, and I'm keeping this one. She wasn't very well for a while after she was born and I want to keep an eye on her for a bit longer. The other two have both been checked by a vet and given all their shots. They are both males, and very healthy little puppies.' She smiled at Molly. 'Do you want to get in there with them and see which one you want to take home?'

Ryan lifted Molly over the barrier, and they left her to play with the puppies while Sheila made tea. She put the two puppies that weren't for sale in a box lined with sheepskin, and after a few minutes they went to sleep curled up together.

'I'm sorry your sister is still in hospital,' Sheila said to Ryan. 'I know she was looking forward to giving Molly the puppy on Christmas morning, but it's probably better this way. If Molly chooses her own pet, she'll realise it's her responsibility. I'll give you a pack of puppy food before you leave.'

They didn't have a puppy carrier, so Ryan bought one from Sheila.

'People who don't already have a dog don't think of things like that,' she said. 'They seem to think they can sit the puppy on their lap for the drive home and it will stay there.'

Molly had already named her puppy Olaf, which evidently had something to do with a film called *Frozen*, so it seemed quite appropriate for this time of the year. The puppy was incredibly cute, with the coat of a Yorkie and the short legs of a dachshund. Molly handled him as if he was made of glass, but Sheila told her he was a tough little dog and well able to stand a bit of rough and tumble.

Once the necessary papers were signed, they loaded Molly and the puppy carrier into the back of the car. 'The dog stays in the basket,' Ryan said firmly. 'This is where you start being a responsible parent. If you let him out and one of us opens the car door, you'll lose him for good.'

The detour to pick up the puppy had cost them all of the extra half hour Fran had allowed, but there was still plenty of time to get to Hazelmere before lunch. Ryan spent most of the time trying to persuade Fran that taking a puppy to her mother's was a very bad idea. In the end Fran suggested they let her mother decide.

'She's a very outspoken woman, Ryan. If she doesn't want the dog in the house, she'll tell you in no uncertain terms, and then we can leave him in an outhouse or something.'

Fran knew her mother lived in a big house — she had lived there herself from the time she was five years old until she moved to London — but she hadn't realised quite how big it might look to someone else until Ryan drove through the iron gates. 'Mansion' was probably too grand a word to use, but the building that stretched in front of them wasn't far off. It was a two-hundred-year-old two-storey manor house with arched windows and an impressive front portico. She had forgotten the place had turrets; they didn't go with the period and were probably a whim of the original builder, but she had loved the look of them when she was a child. She pointed to the open-fronted coach house that was used as a garage.

'I'll let you out first and then park in there next to my mum's car.'

Ryan didn't seem the slightest bit overawed by the size of the house or the parking arrangements. He helped unload the luggage and the puppy basket and then waited while Fran drove her car under cover. By the time she walked back to them, Vanessa had opened the front door.

Fran called out, 'Hi, Mum,' but before she could move Ryan had walked up to Vanessa and kissed her on the cheek.

'It's very kind of you to invite us here for Christmas, Mrs Sutherland. We weren't looking forward to spending it all on our own.'

It was the first time Fran had seen her mother look flustered, but she soon regained her composure. 'So you're Theresa's son, the garage mechanic.'

Ryan took Vanessa's hand in his. He didn't attempt to shake it, just held it. 'My mother lives in Spain. How do you know her, Mrs Sutherland?'

Vanessa smiled. 'We went to school together. I haven't seen her in years, but we keep in touch through the internet. That's how I found out about your predicament.' She looked at Molly, who kept glancing nervously at the dog basket. 'I assume this is Theresa's granddaughter.'

'Yes. Her name is Molly. We're both very grateful for your hospitality.'

He gave Vanessa a dazzling smile as he let go of her hand, and Fran realised he had a dimple she hadn't noticed before. Mind you, he hadn't smiled at her quite like that.

She was beginning to think they might be able to smuggle the puppy in unnoticed, but Olaf must have heard all the voices and got excited. He started to yap and whine both at the same time, and Molly bent down beside the plastic dog-carrier, her face pressed against the grill.

'I think he wants to get out.' She stood up, looking worried. 'And he smells funny.'

No one spoke for a few seconds, and then Vanessa stepped away from the front door and walked towards Molly.

'You have a dog?'

'A puppy dog,' Molly said happily. 'His name is Olaf and he's *my* puppy dog. My mummy bought him for me for Christmas — we just stopped to get him. I have to learn to look after him.'

Vanessa picked up the carrier and peered inside. 'The poor little thing has made quite a mess. I think we need to get him inside the house and clean him up. He must be scared and hungry.' She turned to Ryan. 'Follow me round to the back. We can clean him up in the scullery.

'Can we let him out?' Molly asked as Ryan picked up the carrier. 'He doesn't like it in there.'

Ryan held the carrier at eye level and then quickly moved it to arm's length. He wrinkled his nose. 'Do you have a barn or a stable, Mrs Sutherland? Somewhere Molly can keep the dog until we go home. I can't let him inside if he isn't properly house-trained.'

'I have a barn and a stable, but nothing heated. The poor little thing needs to be somewhere warm. He's just been taken away from his mother. I couldn't allow him to be shut in a cold barn over Christmas.'

Fran thought Ryan might find the prospect of spending Christmas in a barn preferable to spending it with Vanessa, but she had to admit her mother always rose to the occasion. Vanessa couldn't stand to see an animal ill-treated.

The puppy was whisked into the scullery which, in actual fact, was about the size of Fran's living room. It was warm after the temperature outside. Various pieces of horse-riding equipment hung from hooks on the wall, and

Vanessa's designer Wellington boots stood by the door. There was a long counter with a butler sink, a sack of potatoes standing in a corner, and dried herbs hanging from the ceiling. The place smelt of a mixture of horses and herbs — until Ryan put the puppy carrier on the counter, and then the atmosphere changed completely.

Vanessa pulled a gardening apron from one of the hooks and slipped it over her cream silk trouser suit. 'If you look in the shower room over there, Molly, you'll find towels on a shelf. Bring me a big one.'

Fran was already filling the sink with a couple of inches of warm water. She knew the drill. Many a small animal had passed through these doors when she was a child. When she was a small girl she was always rescuing creatures in distress. When she looked at Ryan, Molly, and the smelly puppy in the basket, she realised she had never stopped. It was obviously genetic.

Olaf didn't particularly like his bath.

He howled and shook with fear while Molly hopped around in distress. With his wet fur sticking to him, he looked more like a rat than a dog. Vanessa managed to whip him out of the water and into the towel before he had time to shake himself, and Molly was allowed to rub him dry.

Vanessa took a mobile phone from her pocket and pushed one of the buttons. 'I'm in the scullery, Sarah. Can you organise a meal for a young puppy? Some of the cold chicken will do, but make sure it's cut up very small or give it a second or two in the blender. We also need a cardboard box and one of those old baby blankets.'

'You really don't need to go to all this trouble,' Ryan said. He was obviously grateful to Vanessa, but he looked as if he was getting fed up with having to apologise.

'You can get the dog fed and bedded down and then meet us in the house, Mr Conway. Sarah will show you the way. Fran, you can come with me and help me get the sleeping accommodation sorted out.'

That was her mother's polite way of finding out if she was sleeping with Ryan. Fran grinned at him. 'See you later.' She started to follow her mother, but then turned back. 'By the way, Sarah is my grandmother's housekeeper and companion. She's used to having animals in the scullery.'

As she followed her mother, she smiled to herself. It was tempting to lie about the sleeping arrangements. She would love to see the expression on Ryan's face when he saw they were sharing a double room, but she had a feeling he would be too much of a gentleman to take advantage of the obvious mistake — and that would be too humiliating to risk.

She looked down at herself. Her jeans were covered in dog hairs and her sweater had a damp patch that she decided not to investigate further. She didn't dare think how she smelled. Not of Chanel No. 5, that was for sure.

Right this minute, no man in his right mind would want to take her to bed. A bedroom each would be just fine, and she would suggest they were as far away from one another as possible in case he was tempted to pay her a nocturnal visit. Fat chance of that, she thought ruefully as she hurried to catch up with her mother.

3

Molly was still trying to hold the puppy in the towel. She looked as if she was having trouble, so Ryan took the wriggling animal out of her arms.

'Well,' he said, letting out the breath he had been holding, 'that was a bit of a surprise.'

'I don't want to leave Olaf here by himself,' Molly said, barely suppressing another pout. 'He'll get scared.'

'That'll make two of us, then.' Ryan took another deep breath. 'Mrs Sutherland is a scary lady.'

Molly looked at him is surprise. 'No, she's not. She's nice. She helped me wash Olaf and now she's getting him chicken.'

'We've got puppy food. I left the bag in the car.' He put the little dog down on the tiled floor, where it promptly made a puddle. Ryan ran a hand through his hair. This wasn't going the way he had imagined. He was just looking around frantically for something to wipe the floor with when the door opened and a tall woman with streaks of grey in her hair walked in carrying a cardboard box and a blanket. She gave them both a big smile.

'My name is Sarah; I'm the older Mrs Sutherland's companion. I also help Vanessa run the house. I've been told we have a new puppy. What's his name?'

'Olaf,' Molly said. 'He's just had a bath, but he didn't like it very much.'

'No,' said Sarah, shaking her head, 'puppies don't like having a bath; but because they love muddy puddles they have to have lots of them.' She put the box down next to a radiator. 'I brought him a blanket and a hot water bottle, so he'll be nice and warm. And I minced up some chicken for him, but he can only have a little or it will upset his tummy.'

'I've got puppy food,' Ryan said, 'but

it's out in the car.'

'Go and get it and we can mix it with some of the chicken. That way it will last over the holiday.'

'I don't think Fran locked her car, so it will only take me a minute.'

Ryan left Molly in the more-than-capable hands of Sarah and hurried out to the car. When he got to the coach house, he looked back at the imposing front of the house. For some reason, he had expected a small house in the town of Hazelmere, possibly on a housing estate. Not an impressive manor in several acres of land. It suited Vanessa Sutherland, though. He couldn't imagine her in a small suburban house. Fran didn't fit quite so well, but that was probably because she had moved to London.

He grabbed the bag of puppy food, noticing that Sheila had added a small square of blanket and a knitted toy. Perhaps they would settle Olaf down.

When he got back into the house, Sarah and Molly had already made up

Olaf's bed, but when Ryan added the blanket square and the toy rabbit, the little dog jumped into the makeshift bed with a happy wag of his tail.

'He'll be fine,' Sarah said. 'Puppies get tired very quickly. You can check on him after lunch. I'll show you to your rooms first in case you want to freshen up, but don't be too long. Vanessa's mother-in-law will be joining you for lunch, but Fran's sister and the boys won't get here until later on this evening. They'll be glad to see you and Olaf,' she said to Molly. 'They get bored and want their presents straight away. You'll be a pleasant distraction.'

As she led the way out of the room, Ryan felt Molly slip her hand in his. 'What's a distraction?' she asked a little apprehensively.

'It means a nice surprise,' he told her, 'so make sure you behave yourself at lunch. Fran's grandma will be there, and she's an old lady, so you must be on your best behaviour.'

Molly took her hand back. 'You

always tell me that, Uncle Ryan.'

They passed through a kitchen that was a pleasant mixture of ancient and modern. What looked like the original range stood next to a modern five-burner cooker, and beside the butler sink Ryan could see a state-of-the-art dishwasher. A shiny microwave sat on a marble countertop that had been dulled with a couple of centuries of use, and a rack hanging from the ceiling supported several dented copper saucepans. He would have expected a woman like Vanessa to make a clean sweep and install a modern kitchen in the old house. The fact that she hadn't pleased him immensely.

The hallway — he supposed it was the hallway — was the size of a small ballroom. An enormous Christmas tree took pride of place with a magnificent sweep of a staircase leading up to a minstrel's gallery; the carpet was deep red and obviously not original, but perfectly suited to the dark polished wood of the bannister. He could imagine the ladies, with their hair piled high and jewellery sparkling, descending the stairs slowly to the sound of music and laughter. It would be very easy here to believe in ghosts.

Sarah walked briskly up the stairs in front of them. 'Your cases have already been taken up. I put you in a room next to Molly. There's a connecting door, but you can lock it if you wish.'

'I take it Mr Sutherland is no longer around,' Ryan said, pausing for breath as they reached the landing. He was pretty fit, but he wouldn't want to run up and down this staircase too often in the course of a day.

'No, he isn't,' Sarah said shortly as she opened the door to one of the rooms.

Ryan realised that was all the information he was going to get right now, but Sarah's reluctance to talk about Fran's father intrigued him. Was the man dead, or just missing from the family scene? It was something he intended to find out, even if it was none of his business. He never had been able to resist a mystery.

The connecting door between the rooms was open, and Ryan could see they were similar in size. They looked as if they had recently been refurbished. The predominant colour was blue.

'You each have a small shower room, but if you want a bath you might have to join a queue in the morning.' Sarah looked at her watch. 'Vanessa will expect you downstairs in about fifteen minutes, so it might be best to unpack later.' She looked back as she reached the door. 'I'll check on your puppy, Molly, but I expect he's still asleep. You can visit him after lunch.'

Ryan had to admit he was a little out of his depth. There wasn't time for more than a quick freshen-up, so he hoped the clothes they had arrived in would be suitable attire for lunch with Vanessa and her mother-in-law. He tried to remember what Vanessa had been wearing. He was pretty sure the woman's long, elegant legs had been clad in blue denim, so jeans were probably OK; but was a long-sleeved T-shirt emblazoned with the Ferrari logo a bit too casual? He looked down. From that angle, the prancing horse looked a bit sissy. Perhaps he should have gone for the raging bull of Lamborghini.

Molly came back into his room and then it was too late to change anything. The little girl looked pretty enough to him, but how to dress a five-year-old had never been high on his list of things to learn.

He started down the staircase wondering which way to go once they reached the bottom, but he needn't have worried as Fran was there to greet them. He thought again how stunning she managed to look without even trying. She had tied her tangle of dark coppery curls on top of her head, which made him think of his ladies on the staircase; but a few tendrils had escaped to curl unnoticed in front of her ears, giving her a slightly tousled look. She came towards him with a warm smile.

'I thought you might lose your way. This house is too damned big for its own good. Certainly far too big for Mum and Grandma, even with Sarah to help out.'

He smiled back at her. 'Not a problem. I'm quite good at finding my way around strange places.'

Molly was already heading across the hall towards an open door. 'Mummy says if you get lost in someone's house, you go where the noise is coming from.'

'See?' Ryan said. 'No problem.' He caught up with Molly and took her hand. 'Wait for me, please, Molly. I might get scared if you leave me on my own.'

The little girl giggled. 'You never get scared, Uncle Ryan.'

He did get scared sometimes, he thought as he let Molly guide him towards the murmur of voices. Women like Fran, who made his heart give a little skip every time he laid eyes on her, scared him silly.

There were only two people in the

room: Vanessa, with a glass in her hand, and a white-haired lady sitting very upright in a high-backed chair. A log fire was burning in a brick fireplace, spitting and hissing to itself and smelling of pine, and a round table had been set with silver and crystal. Against one wall a long sideboard held covered dishes that filled the room with an enticing smell of food.

Molly stopped in the doorway and Ryan heard her give a little gasp of pleasure. In front of the window another large Christmas tree held pride of place. The gold star on top skimmed the high ceiling and fairy lights twinkled and flashed. The decorations were all red and gold: baubles, stars and strings of shiny beads, with crystal icicles dripping from the branches. The overall effect was magical.

Ryan watched Molly walk slowly towards the tree and look up at the star. He saw her give a little shiver of excitement before she turned to give him a smile of pure delight, and in that instant Ryan realised why people have children. A Christmas tree can only truly be seen through the eyes of a child.

Vanessa turned and motioned them into the room. 'Good, you're here at last. We waited for you so we can have a drink before we eat, and so I can introduce you to my mother-in-law. Annabel, this is Ryan Conway. He's Theresa's son. I invited Ryan and his niece to stay with us for the Christmas holiday. He came with Francesca.'

Ryan raised an eyebrow. Francesca? He grinned at Fran and she scowled back at him. He took the glass of champagne Vanessa put in his hand and turned his attention to the woman in the chair. He had been expecting . . . well, whatever he had been expecting, Fran's granny wasn't it. The woman's face was lined, but her eyes were bright and shrewd, enhanced cleverly with a touch of eyeshadow and mascara. She was wearing a dress in muted pinks and mauves and her pure white hair was cut in a flattering style that reminded him of pictures of Jane Fonda. No little old lady this, but a beautiful lady of the manor.

She held out her hand and Ryan wasn't sure whether to shake it or kiss it, so he did neither. He just held her delicate hand in his for a few seconds before letting go.

Annabel smiled at him. 'I think I know you, Mr Conway. I'm sure we've met before.'

Ryan shook his head. 'If we'd met before, I would definitely remember.'

Fran appeared beside him. 'Ryan is a garage mechanic, Grandma, so unless you've been having trouble with your car recently, I very much doubt you've met him before.'

Ryan frowned. He didn't think she was trying to put him down. She seemed to dislike everything to do with the opulence around her, and a garage mechanic and a small child probably outdid her mother when it came to helping the needy. He had a feeling that if he had been a good-looking multi-millionaire, he would have been left behind in London.

Sarah appeared at the door. 'If we're all here, I suggest we eat. Our guests must be starving.'

Once the lids were removed from the dishes on the sideboard, Ryan realised this was no ordinary buffet lunch. Molly didn't look impressed. She had probably been hoping for pizza and chips, something she would cheerfully consume for every meal. She shuddered in horror at the look of the duck breast with its crispy skin, and eventually put a couple of crab croquettes on her plate before adding a spoonful of sauteed potato.

'What are these?' she whispered to Ryan, pointing to the croquettes.

'Fishcakes,' he told her. 'And those are fried potatoes, a bit like chips. Try the carrots, Molly. They've been cooked in butter.'

'I don't like carrots. Why aren't there any peas?' she complained fretfully. 'We always have peas at home.'

He sat his niece at the table next to Fran and dropped into a chair on the other side so Molly was between them. Maybe that way he could keep her out of trouble. The food was delicious, and Ryan wondered whether it was catered or if Sarah and Vanessa managed the whole thing by themselves. When he asked, Fran told him it was a bit of both.

'The meat and fish get delivered from a local hotel, and Sarah sorts out the vegetables. We have quite a respectable vegetable plot, or we used to when I lived at home. Chickens too, at one time. Grandma Annabel is a bit of a pain where food is concerned, but if she has enough to drink, she's not so fussy.'

He looked across the table and noticed Annabel was already on her second glass of wine. Molly tried her fishcakes and decided she liked them, so that was another worry out of the way. He was beginning to enjoy himself and couldn't wait to meet the rest of the family.

Fran was pleased to see Ryan so relaxed. She hadn't been sure how he would fit in. Vanessa was the quintessential do-gooder and Annabel was a social snob, but he seemed quite at ease with both of them. Vanessa mentioned an eating place in Cannes she had visited last year, and looked slightly puzzled when Ryan recommended a Michelin-starred restaurant in the Old Town.

'Expensive,' he said, 'but worth every euro.'

For a moment Fran wondered if he was making it up to impress, but it didn't sound that way.

'We have met before,' Annabel said. 'I'm sure of it. Maybe in Paris or somewhere like that. We obviously frequent the same places.'

'Possibly. I get the job of delivering a car over in France sometimes.' He smiled at her, showing his dimple again. 'But if we had met before, I'm sure I would have remembered. I don't often forget a beautiful woman.'

They finished the meal with coffee in the drawing room, where floor-to-ceiling windows showed the formal gardens outside. The herbaceous borders and containers were looking a little bedraggled at the moment, but in the summer they were a riot of colour. Fran remembered she had once had her own little flowerbed filled with plants grown from the seeds she collected. They didn't always come up as expected, because she liked weeds as much as cultivated plants, but it had always been fun, particularly when her father had been around to laugh at her mix of dandelions and hybrid aquilegia. Her daddy told her the pretty coloured flowers were called columbine, and when you looked closely you could see swans sitting in a circle.

She bit her lip in annoyance. That's why she didn't like coming home for Christmas. It always brought back too many memories.

Molly squeezed into the armchair beside her. 'When can we have our presents? Do we have to wait until tomorrow, or can we have them tonight?'

'The boys haven't arrived yet. I tell you what — it's stopped raining so why don't we wrap up warm and go for a walk outside? There's a tree house and a secret garden.'

Molly's eyes opened wide. 'A tree house? Is that a house in a tree? Can I go in it? And what's a secret garden? Why is it a secret?'

Fran laughed. 'So I take it that's a yes to my suggestion. Shall we ask Uncle Ryan to go with us?'

'If you want. Can we take Olaf? He'd love to go for a walk.'

'Not today. I think he's too tired to go out, and it's very cold; he's probably still asleep at the moment. But maybe tomorrow. When we come back, you can go and see him and give him some more chicken.'

Ryan met them at the bottom of the stairs wearing a duffle and desert boots. Fran had helped Molly wrap up warm enough for a walk round the garden and borrowed a pair of her mother's wellies for herself. She was finding the idea of showing Ryan and Molly around her old haunts quite exciting. A visit home usually turned into a disaster. There was still time for that to happen, she told herself, and it probably would, but for the moment she was having fun.

The gardens around the house extended to a couple of acres, plus a small area of woodland and a three-acre meadow that also belonged to them. There was still a pair of stables and a paddock, even though they no longer kept any horses. Her grandmother had competed in dressage competitions and still joined in the local hunt, although they no longer chased foxes. Fran had been given a pony when she was two years old. That was when her father had decided she was old enough to learn to ride. She remembered how sad she had been when she grew too big for Florence and the little pony had to be sold.

She was pleased to see there were still

a few chickens in the henhouse, probably looked after by Sarah. Sarah had been with the family before Fran was born, and none of them could have survived without her help. She was still an essential part of their lives.

Molly made a beeline for the chicken run, but she had never been close to live chickens before and found the noisy, flapping birds a little scary.

'Tomorrow you can help me collect the eggs for breakfast,' Fran said. 'The chickens will be quieter then.'

'No thank you,' Molly said politely. 'Can we see the tree house, please?'

Ryan grinned at Fran. 'I think children are born single-minded. Once Molly gets her teeth into something, she won't leave it alone.' He wiped a gloved hand across his face and looked up at the sky. 'That's not rain. It's sleet.'

'It's snowing, it's snowing!' Molly sang, dancing along in front of them.

'No, your uncle is right — it's sleet,' said Fran. 'Horrid cold, wet stuff. Perhaps we should go back.'

Molly turned round, her face screwed up in a scowl. 'I want to see the treehouse. You promised.'

Fran closed her eyes and took a deep breath. She had suggested this expedition, and she had promised Molly a look at the treehouse. She just hoped it was still there. She hadn't been on this part of the estate for years and years.

Molly saw it first. It sat in the branches of the old oak tree just as Fran remembered, the rope ladder hanging down almost to the ground. Her father had called in a local craftsman and he had created something that looked as if it should be halfway up the mast of a pirate ship, but the two girls had loved it. It made Fran smile just to look at it, and she wondered why she had stayed away so long. Even in a shower of rain and sleet, the little wooden house looked magical.

Before they could stop her, Molly had taken a run at the ladder and was halfway up before Ryan could tell to her to come down. He looked at Fran worriedly. 'Is it safe?'

She shook her head. 'I don't know. It was when I used to play in it with Lucy, but that was years ago.' She added her voice to Ryan's, calling to the little girl to come down, but Molly just laughed and climbed the rest of the way to the wooden decking and then hauled herself up into the house. The next moment her head popped out of a window.

'Look at me! I'm the king of the castle!'

'Come down now, Molly,' Fran repeated. 'It may not be safe up there.'

Ryan still looked worried and Fran wasn't surprised. The house was a lot further from the ground than she remembered. 'And we have to see the secret garden before it gets dark,' she called. 'You can come back again and play in the house when we've made sure it's safe.'

Molly appeared in the doorway and looked over the side at the ground below. 'I can't get down,' she said. 'I don't know how.'

4

Fran had a sudden flashback to the first time she had come down the rope ladder. It was fine going up, but coming down was something else altogether, and back then it had been a lovely midsummer day.

'Hold on to the bottom of the ladder,' she told Ryan. 'We need to stop it swinging.' She put her foot on the bottom rung to help Ryan hold it firm and looked up at Molly. 'Turn around until you're facing backwards, and feel for the first rung with your foot. If you hold on tight to the sides of the rail, you'll be fine.'

Molly turned her back on them, held on to the rail, and waved a foot around in the air. 'I can't feel it.'

'She's not going to do it, is she?' Ryan said. 'I'll have to go up and get her.'

Fran looked at him. All six feet something of him. Most of it muscle. 'How much do you weigh?' She didn't wait for his answer. 'A lot more than me, I bet. That ladder will never hold your weight, Ryan, and if it breaks we'll never get her down. Stay where you are,' she called out to Molly. 'I'm coming up to get you.'

Her plan had been to go halfway up and coax Molly to follow her down. But the best-laid plans never work. She even reached up and tried holding one of Molly's legs to guide her foot to the first rung of the ladder, but all she got was a kick that just missed her face and nearly knocked her off the ladder. She wished she could just grab the child round the waist and pull her off the deck, but that would have them both tumbling to the ground.

Plan B started off all right. Fran took off her gloves and threw them down to Ryan. Then she climbed the rest of the way up and joined Molly on the deck, hoping the old, possibly rotten wood could take their combined weight. She got Molly to lie on her stomach and held the little girl by her wrists. Feeling safer, Molly wriggled herself over the edge and got her feet on the first rung of the ladder. She got halfway down and then stopped again.

'Just a little bit further,' Ryan called from below, 'and I can reach you.'

Fran watched him catch Molly, and when he set her on the ground she breathed a sigh of relief. Now all she had to do was get down herself. 'Just hold the damn ladder steady,' she called down. 'It used to scare me silly when it swung around all over the place.'

Making sure he had a firm grip on the ladder below, she turned her back on him and lowered herself over the side. She had only stepped onto the first rung when she heard a ripping sound. She barely stifled a scream. It wasn't just a rung of the rope ladder that had broken: the whole thing had ripped away from the treehouse, and there wasn't anything she could do about it. Unable to see what was going on below, she hung by her fingertips from the decking for a few seconds before she shut her eyes and let go.

Ryan managed to catch her in his arms, but her weight knocked him over and he let out a whoosh of air as they both hit the ground with him underneath. She rolled off him as quickly as she could and stood up on shaky legs.

'Are you all right?'

He shook his head weakly, trying to take a breath, and she wondered if she should give him the kiss of life. The ground beneath him was soggy from the rain and padded with a layer of old leaves, so she doubted he was seriously hurt, but he had just saved her life and she felt she owed him something. As he pushed himself slowly to his feet, she stood on tiptoe and kissed him on his cold cheek. 'Thank you.'

Once Molly knew they were both fine, she started giggling. They must have looked quite funny, Fran thought, as she dropped out of the tree and knocked Ryan flat on his back. Not the sort of entertainment she had planned for the afternoon, but it had obviously amused the child.

'Perhaps you aren't the featherweight you thought you were,' Ryan said, rubbing his backside. 'I've had women throw themselves at me before, but they don't usually completely bowl me over.'

'Ha funny ha,' Fran said, as she brushed herself down. They were both soaking wet and dirty, and the sleet had turned into sharp little bits of ice that stung when they hit her face. All she wanted to do was get inside and take a hot shower.

'Is it snowing?' Molly asked hopefully. 'It looks like snow.'

'Not proper snow,' Ryan said as they headed back towards the house. 'But it's getting colder, so it could still be a white Christmas. Maybe when you wake up in the morning, there will be snow everywhere.'

'We haven't been to the secret garden yet,' Molly complained.

'The secret garden will have to wait for another day,' Fran said firmly. 'We need to get inside and get warmed up, and you've got to feed your puppy. It's a good job we didn't bring him with us. He wouldn't like this nasty sleety stuff, would he?'

They were even wetter by the time they reached the warmth of the kitchen. Sarah helped Molly off with her outdoor clothes and gave Fran and Ryan a curious look. 'I can't imagine you were doing anything you shouldn't, not in front of the child, but you both look as if you've been rolling on the ground.'

'We have,' Ryan said with a smile. 'But not for the reasons that seem to be going through your head. Our little roll in the woods was completely above-board.'

'Fran fell out of the tree house,' Molly offered helpfully. 'She fell on top of Uncle Ryan and they both fell in the mud.'

Sarah just raised an eyebrow. 'That

sounds like fun,' she said. 'Why don't you all go upstairs and have a hot bath or shower before you change for dinner. I'll check on Olaf and see he gets fed.' She turned to Fran. 'I need to speak to you for a minute.'

Ryan took Molly by the hand. 'I'll take this dirty child upstairs and make sure she has a shower. I've discovered she can manage a shower on her own without drowning.'

Once they had left the kitchen, Sarah glared at Fran. 'You took Molly to the tree house? What on earth were you thinking? No one has looked at that ramshackle contraption for years. It probably isn't safe.'

'No, it isn't,' Fran replied dryly. 'I proved that when the ladder broke. But no one got hurt as far as I know, although Ryan might be a little bruised. I'm surprised the boys haven't found it.'

'That's because they're not allowed anywhere near it.' Sarah pulled a face and sighed. 'And that's a pity, isn't it? I know how much fun you used to have with your sister in the tree house, and the twins would love it. I'll get someone to come over once the weather gets better and see if it can be made safe again.'

Fran followed Sarah into the scullery, where a dozy puppy climbed out of his box and tentatively wagged a tail that looked too long for his little body. Fran knelt on the floor and he licked the hand she held out to him. 'Is he OK? He looks a bit sad.'

'I'll give him some more food and water and he'll be fine.' Sarah gathered up the newspaper she had laid on the floor in a corner of the room. 'He's partly housetrained, but everything is very strange for him at the moment so he's bound to have accidents. Perhaps tomorrow he can have a little run outside. I'm sure we've got a collar and lead around somewhere.'

'Thank you, Sarah. I'm sorry to lumber you with all this. Mum always seems to get out of any hard work.'

Sarah smiled. 'She has the house

cleaned from top to bottom once a month by a cleaning firm, but she wouldn't want me to tell you that. She does her bit, though, Fran. She copes with all the bills and things on the computer in the office — I'm useless at figures, you know that — and she organises things like this Christmas get-together.' She patted Fran on the arm. 'We make a good team, me and your mum, and Annabel helps us keep up appearances. I think she wears her diamonds to bed.'

Fran laughed. 'I'll go and have a shower and change my clothes.' She started towards the door and then turned back. 'I didn't bring anything posh to wear tomorrow.'

Sarah looked at her thoughtfully. 'You never do. It's a shame, though. That good-looking young man you brought with you might like to see you in a dress.'

Fran scowled. She wasn't going to change the habits of a lifetime, but she wished she'd packed her cashmere dress. It wasn't the first time her stubbornness had been her downfall. Her father had left her mother on that Christmas Day many years ago, but he had left his daughters as well. No one had ever told her why he left, and she had always been too pig-headed to ask. At the back of her mind, that little niggling doubt would always remain. Had his abrupt departure had anything to do with her? Lucy was five years older and always well-behaved, but Fran had been the naughty one. Had she behaved so badly he couldn't bear to be in the same house as a naughty child, even if that naughty child was his own daughter?

She had changed into black jeggings and a long burgundy top and was brushing her hair, trying to decide what to do with it, when she heard a commotion downstairs: the sound of the two boys squabbling, her sister shouting, and her brother-in-law's deep voice rising above the others as he tried to calm them all down.

Fran gave up on her hair; it really didn't matter what she did with it. No one was likely to notice. As soon as Lucy and the boys arrived, chaos reigned, and it would remain like that until they left again. Add Molly to the mix, and life should get even more interesting. She was just thanking the powers that be that she only had to submit to this torture once or twice a year, when her bedroom door burst open.

'There are people downstairs. Is that your sister? Are the boys here? Can we open our presents now they've come?'

Fran looked at Ryan, who had followed his niece and was now standing in her bedroom doorway. 'Does she only ask questions?'

'Pretty much. That's the way kids find out things.'

'Is that so? Perhaps I should try that.' She looked at him thoughtfully. He was wearing black cord trousers and a soft sweater a shade darker his eyes. He looked, she thought, almost good

67

enough to eat. 'Are you married?' she asked him, deciding on a direct approach.

'No. Nor am I engaged or seeing anyone special at this time. So I'm completely free of any liabilities and encumbrances at the moment, and readily available for anything you may have in mind. I take that back,' he said, looking at Molly. 'I have one liability, but she is only temporary.'

Fran laughed. 'That's part of my family making all that noise downstairs, so I seem to have a lot more liabilities and encumbrances than you. Normally the boys take over the house at Christmas, but perhaps we have a secret weapon in Molly.'

Ryan pursed his lips. 'She might be able to defeat them with questions. She's capable of a veritable barrage once she gets going. Shall we go downstairs and see how it works out?'

Molly was already halfway down the wide staircase, hopping from one foot to the other while she waited for them to catch up. She had dressed herself in a red woollen dress and pale pink leggings. An interesting combination, Fran thought, but anything Ryan might have suggested would have been over-ruled by his niece.

'Can I show them my puppy?'

'Later, maybe,' Ryan said. 'And only under strict supervision. That little dog is your responsibility, and you don't want him to be scared, do you? Besides, it might be a good idea to say hello first.'

The boys had grown, Fran thought, and she wondered how that could have happened in a few months. She had seen them all at Easter, but then she realised that was eight months ago. How could she have let it go so long without a visit to her mother or her sister? The twins were her nephews, and she always meant to keep in touch, but somehow the time just slipped away.

Both the boys were blond and fair-skinned like their mother, a gene that must have come from their father's side of the family. Her mother's hair had been the colour of black coffee at one time; now it was a shade or two lighter and streaked with a whisper of grey, but cleverly cut to make the most of her aristocratic cheekbones. Fran lifted a hand to her own face. The cheekbone gene must have got lost in the shuffle somewhere because she certainly hadn't inherited it.

In the momentary silence that greeted their arrival in the hallway, Molly studied the boys with interest. 'You both look the same,' she said. 'How do you know which one of you is which?'

'We have different names,' George said.

Molly nodded as if that explained everything. 'Good,' she said. 'Do we get to open our presents now?'

Ryan rolled his eyes and smiled at Lucy. 'I'm sorry, I should have introduced myself. I know you're Fran's sister, and I presume this is your husband. My name is Ryan, and Mrs Sutherland kindly asked us here for the Christmas holiday. This is my niece, Molly. She's five years old. Six in February.'

Lucy took his outstretched hand. 'It's nice to meet you, Ryan. This is my husband, Richard, and the boys are George and Eric. They're just seven.'

Richard waved a hand in the air above the boys' heads. 'Hi, Ryan. Glad to meet you.'

Fran gave her sister an awkward hug and then stepped back. 'My goodness! I thought the boys had grown, but just look at you. Should you be travelling? You must be due any minute.'

Lucy laughed. 'Not until after Christmas, I hope. I've got another two weeks to go yet, and anyway we had to come here to be with you all. The boys look forward to it.' She smiled at Ryan. 'Mum and Sarah put on the best Christmas ever, and I have trouble coping with cooking at the moment.'

'Cooking makes her feel sick,' Richard said by way of explanation, 'but eating doesn't. I don't think anything ever puts

Lucy off her food.'

Lucy gave her husband a playful punch on the arm. 'Have you seen all the Christmas trees yet?' she asked Molly. 'We always have three. We've had three trees in this house for as long as I can remember.'

Molly held up her hand and counted on her fingers. 'There's this big one here in the hall.' She gazed up at the huge tree again. 'And there's one in the room where we had our lunch.' She looked down at her hand. 'That's only two. Where's the other one?'

'The other one is in the grand room, and no one goes in there until tomorrow,' Vanessa said. 'You know I like to keep the decorations in there a secret until Christmas Day.'

Sarah, who had been standing quietly to one side, held up a key. 'I locked the door so no one can creep in.' She frowned at George and Eric. 'That happened last year, didn't it, and spoiled the surprise.'

'We wanted to see if we had any presents,' Eric said. 'We're not allowed to even look at them until Christmas morning,' he told Molly, 'and we wanted to make sure there were some for us under the tree.'

'You rattled them and poked them until the wrapping started to come off. It's a wonder they weren't all broken by the time you opened them.'

Molly pulled a face. 'I don't like having to wait. I'm always allowed to open mine before I go to bed. Mummy says it stops me waking up too early on Christmas morning.'

Sarah laughed. 'But the boys know they can't get in the room before breakfast, so there's no point in them waking up early.'

Lucy and her husband took the boys upstairs to unpack and freshen up, and Vanessa suggested they have a pre-dinner drink while the boys were out of the way. 'Annabel is already in the drawing room pouring her first cocktail, so I need to keep an eye on her. I usually make her a few alcohol-free ones,' she told Ryan. 'If she's already had a couple, she doesn't notice any difference.'

Fran knew her grandmother had banned the bomb and burned her bra and walked around London on marches when she was younger, and she had evidently smoked like a chimney as well before Vanessa and Sarah moved in with the children. She gave up smoking without an argument, because Vanessa told her it would harm her granddaughters, but now she seemed to have taken a liking to alcohol instead.

As soon as Fran walked through the door, her grandmother beckoned her over. 'Come and sit beside me, Francesca. I want to know all about the young man you brought with you.'

'I don't know anything about him,' Fran said. 'Mum invited him. She told me he was the son of a friend of hers and having to look after his niece over Christmas. All I know is that he's not married and he's a garage mechanic.' She looked across at Ryan. 'I thought he might be out of his depth, but he seems to be doing fine.'

Annabel smoothed her dress over her knees. Fran knew she was almost eighty, but she looked at least ten years younger. She was wearing a cream silk dress with a high neckline, a diamond necklace, and drop earrings. Fran only vaguely remembered her granddad, but she knew he had adored Annabel and showered her with expensive jewellery all her life. Better than life insurance, he told her; but when he died he left her the house and enough money to live comfortably for the rest of her life. She never did have to sell her diamonds.

Fran looked round the beautiful room and wondered why she struggled to earn her living in London when she could have stayed here. But she knew the answer. She had no intention of marrying a millionaire like her grandmother. Someone had once told her that nothing is worth having unless you've earned it, and so that was what she was doing. Earning her independence.

Ryan was standing by the fireplace chatting to Vanessa and Molly. He looked completely at home, and not for the first time she wondered if he really was a garage mechanic. He had told her his flat was over the place where he worked, and she had imagined some sort of loft over a smelly garage, but now she was beginning to wonder.

At that moment there was a noise outside, and the twins ran into the room closely followed by Richard. Lucy waddled along behind, a hand on her stomach. She still managed to look attractive, Fran thought, even with a bump as big as a house and flat shoes on her swollen feet.

Lucy kissed her grandmother on the cheek. 'Don't get up, Grandma. I'll come and sit beside you.' She puffed out a breath. 'Sitting in the car with a seat belt on is quite uncomfortable, but I have to wear it unless I'm actually in labour.' She eased herself down on to the sofa beside Annabel. 'And I've told this little one she has to stay where she is for another couple of weeks.'

'So you know what you're having.' Ryan said.

Lucy nodded happily. 'I'm really pleased it's a little girl. I know if it had been another baby boy, I'd fall in love with him as soon as I saw him. But a baby girl will make our family complete.'

Richard had come to stand beside his wife. 'At least we know there's only one in there this time.'

Lucy smiled up at him. 'I rather fancied two little girls.'

Annabel patted her hand. 'I wish your father could be here to see his grandchildren. I'm sure he'd like to, but Australia is so far away. He always asks about the boys when he emails me. He said something about skype, but I don't know what that is.'

'If he actually thinks I'm going to . . . ' Lucy began, her face flushing with colour, but Richard had been standing next to her and he put a hand on her shoulder.

'Remember it's Christmas, Lucy, my love. And besides, you mustn't get upset about anything at the moment.'

5

'Can I get anyone a drink?' Ryan asked diplomatically. He walked across the room to the little bar he had noticed in the corner, and when he turned around he saw Sarah had followed him. He gave her a grateful smile: 'I expect you know what everyone wants better than I do, but I can do the pouring if you like.'

'Annabel has always had a habit of saying the wrong thing at the wrong time, but she does it more often these days. I think we had better dilute her vodka martini a little. Nothing for Lucy, of course, and Vanessa will want a Manhattan.'

Ryan picked up a bottle of Canadian whisky. 'Half and half?'

Sarah laughed. 'Yes, go on then. She looks as if she needs a strong one.'

He topped up the glass with vermouth and added a dash of bitters.

'How about Fran? I only met her a few hours ago, so I have no idea what she drinks.'

'Not a lot, usually, but she'll have a tall glass of vodka and tonic with ice.' Sarah put her hand on his arm. 'Hang around for a while if you can, Ryan. I think you'll be good for her. All she does at the moment is work.'

He mixed himself a scotch and soda, picked up Fran's glass, and walked over to where she was sitting with Annabel and Lucy.

'I'm sorry,' Lucy said apologetically. 'It doesn't take much to upset me at the moment.'

Ryan laughed. 'I'd be more than upset if I had a seven- or eight-pound baby inside me. I think that was a design fault. A backpack would have worked much better.'

'Sleeping might be a problem, though.' She grinned at him. 'Mind you, it would be lovely to take it off at night and hang it over the back of a chair.'

Molly came running over, followed by the boys. 'Can we go and see Olaf? Sarah says she'll come with us.'

'Just for half an hour,' Sarah said. 'I'll make sure they all wash their hands before dinner.'

'Are you sure, Sarah?' Ryan felt guilty about leaving Molly with her; the poor woman seemed to have enough to cope with already. 'Would you like me to come as well?'

She shook her head. 'No, I miss having kids around, and the puppy needs to play for a little while. I'll make sure he doesn't get too excited. Molly can give him his last feed and we'll tuck him up for the night.'

Ryan sat in a chair next to Richard and took a sip of his drink. 'I admire the way you handle your two boys. I'm having trouble with one little girl.'

'The boys are nearly seven years old, so I've had plenty of practice. Vanessa told me you work in a garage, Ryan. Do you sell cars, or just do repairs?'

'We do restoration work mostly. Then

we have to sell them. Most of the good ones finish up abroad, which is a shame.'

Ryan saw Richard's eyes light up. 'Vintage or classic? That must be a fantastic job. What are you working on at the moment?'

'A Bentley Continental. I took it out for a run a couple of days ago. It's a fantastic car.'

Vanessa joined them with a drink in each hand. She handed one to her mother-in-law. 'Your boss let you take a Bentley out for a joy ride, Ryan? I hope you're a good driver.'

When he didn't comment, Annabel leant back on the sofa and smiled at him. 'I shall remember how I know you eventually. It just takes me a little longer these days. I believe someone said a brain is like a computer. I think I must have a slow connection speed.'

'You need to change your service provider, Grandma,' Lucy said with a laugh.

'I may be a bit slow,' she said, looking

at Vanessa, 'but my alcohol detection device is still working perfectly, and this drink is completely lacking in anything that goes by that name.' She smiled sweetly at Ryan and handed him her glass. 'Could you throw this concoction away and get me a proper drink, Ryan? A vodka martini would be nice. And please don't forget the vodka this time.'

Ryan decided he had fallen in love with Annabel. She was a wonderful old lady. So what if she got a bit tipsy? He would have thought she was entitled to do what she liked in her own house, particularly at Christmas. He felt like adding double the amount of vodka to her drink, just for fun, but that wouldn't be fair on Annabel.

He glanced across the room at Fran. She was sitting next to Lucy, and the two women were laughing about something. The sisters bore a family resemblance; but whereas Fran was dark with a hint of copper in her unruly curls, Lucy had straight fair hair the colour of milky coffee, and pale skin. Technically, Lucy was probably the prettier of the two girls; but Fran had something about her, something he couldn't quite put his finger on. The way she scorned her family's lifestyle amused him. If times had been different, she would probably have gone to Paris and found a garret in Montmartre. As it was, she lived in a rented apartment no bigger than her grandmother's scullery, and obviously hated the opulence of this beautiful house. He wondered what she would make of his own apartment.

He felt blessed to have been invited to share this family Christmas. It was something neither he nor his sister had managed to achieve for a number of years. They always made an effort, mainly for Molly, but nothing could replace the father she had lost, and Christmas brought back memories for both of them.

There were things about this family that piqued his curiosity. There had to be an explanation for Annabel's insistence that she knew him. He was convinced he had never sold her a car. He certainly didn't recognise either of the vehicles that had been parked in the coach house when they arrived — and he still wanted to know what had happened to Fran's father. The man was obviously still alive if he was corresponding with Annabel by email.

He noticed that all the women had made an effort to dress up for dinner tonight, and he had a feeling Christmas lunch was going to be quite a formal affair. He was annoyed with Fran for not warning him when she came to pick him up, but glad to see Richard was also casually dressed. Lucy's husband was wearing grey chinos and a black sweater with a v-neck. Ryan liked the man. He had shown he was able to handle boisterous twins and a pregnant wife without too much trouble, and Ryan felt that was an accomplishment to be admired. As he had told Richard, he was having enough trouble managing Molly.

Thinking about his niece reminded

him he needed to phone the hospital. If Karen was out of danger and feeling better, the least he could do was wish her a happy Christmas, even if she *had* lumbered him with her daughter and an incontinent puppy. He had managed to get hold of a signed copy of the latest book by her favourite author and left it at the hospital. Perhaps when she was well enough they could do the Orlando trip Molly had been asking for. Seeing Lucy and Richard together had made him realise how much Karen must miss the husband she had loved so much. He wondered if that sort of love would ever come his way. He knew he would never settle for less.

Sarah came back with the children and laughingly wiped a hand across her brow. 'I had forgotten how tiring children can be. Throw an excitable puppy into the mix and things get a bit chaotic. I had also forgotten I am a little bit older now.' She held up a hand when Ryan started to say something. 'But I wouldn't have missed it for the world. Thank you for bringing Molly and Olaf into our lives, Ryan. She is a remarkable little girl. She sorted the boys out in no time, telling them they had to be gentle with Olaf and not to run around so much because they would frighten him.'

'I'll check on dinner,' Vanessa said. 'We're eating a little earlier than usual so the children can join us. This is a family gathering, and eating together is a family pastime.' She aimed a look at Fran. 'It's a pity we can't do it more often.'

'That would be lovely, Mother, but some of us have to work for a living.'

Ryan winced, waiting for Vanessa's comeback. He had a feeling she wouldn't let her daughter beat her at a game of rhetoric.

'If you only define work as paid employment, Francesca — something that must have a monetary reward at the end — then it's a shame you feel the need to do it.'

She left the room slowly and with

great elegance, leaving Fran looking a little foolish — maybe, Ryan thought, even a little embarrassed. He wanted to go over and put his arms round her, and wondered where on earth that thought had come from. Probably from the moment she fell on him in the woods and he had felt the soft weight of her body on his. Even the cold mud he was lying in didn't stop a few erotic thoughts entering his head.

She looked as if she had made an effort tonight, with tight velvet trousers and a toffee-coloured top. Still casual, but on Fran absolutely stunning. She had left her hair loose, falling to her shoulders in soft curls that gleamed bronze in the light of the chandelier. He remembered the colour of her eyes almost matched her hair, amber with a touch of gold. They had been only inches from his when she was lying on top of him. The bones in her face were too strong to give her the soft prettiness of her sister, but he had a feeling she wasn't as tough as she made out. He had noticed a slight tremble in her bottom lip before Vanessa left the room.

The meal passed uneventfully. Molly was on her best behaviour, and the boys appeared to have worn themselves out playing with the puppy. Seeing the children together made Ryan realise how grown-up Molly was for her age. She was sitting beside Annabel and leant over to whisper something in the old lady's ear that made her laugh out loud. Ryan saw they were both looking across the table at the twins. George had tomato sauce round his mouth and on the tip of his nose, probably from scooping up ketchup with a roast potato, and Eric was crawling around under the table looking for his missing napkin.

Richard was about to say something to them, but Lucy beat him to it. A few remarks about Christmas presents only being delivered to good children soon had the desired effect. George wiped his mouth and picked up his knife and fork, and Eric crawled out from under the table and anchored his napkin in the waistband of his trousers.

Once peace was restored, Ryan turned his attention to Fran. She was sitting beside him, but she had been quiet throughout most of the meal. She must have felt his eyes on her, because she turned to look at him. She was close enough for him to smell a hint of perfume.

'Thank you,' he said quietly, 'for bringing me here. I know I have Vanessa to thank for the invitation, but I shall remember this Christmas for the rest of my life.'

'People who spend Christmas with us often say that,' she said with a smile. 'Christmases at this house are usually quite memorable.'

'Why don't you like coming here?' he asked curiously. 'Your mother seems a nice enough woman, and I adore your grandmother. Lucy and her husband are lovely, and the boys are . . . boys.'

'My mother is on her best behaviour. She always is when new people are around. Most of the time she's a control freak.' Fran sighed. 'To be fair, I suppose she had to be when our father left. She managed on her own for nearly a year. I was five when he went, and Lucy was ten. Mother had never worked in her life. She had no idea how to earn a living. She got odd jobs but it wasn't enough to pay the mortgage, so she sold the house and we all went to live with Grandma. Sarah was already living with Grandma as a live-in housekeeper/companion, so she took over looking after us as well. I think she actually likes children.'

He felt his eyebrow go up. 'And you don't?'

'Don't sound so surprised. Not every woman wants a house full of screaming brats. Some of us quite like working for a living, whatever my mother may think.'

She turned her head away, but Ryan studied her thoughtfully. He didn't believe her. She had talked herself into being the epitome of the young, successful businesswoman and then made herself believe that was what she really wanted. But the way she behaved with Molly and her exuberant nephews didn't give him the impression she hated children. Besides, a lot of women coped quite successfully with both children and a career.

He thought Fran probably had to dress up for work every day and looked forward to getting out of her smart suits and high heels, but her mother insisted on a dress code at Christmas and Fran resented it, so she rebelled. He imagined she had been the rebellious one all her life. Lucy, with her soft prettiness and gentle nature, must have been a hard act to follow. Particularly when she'd found herself a good-looking, successful husband and had two lovely children.

Resentment could be corrosive and eat away at the heart of you; Ryan knew that from experience. He had resented the fact that his father had died in his early sixties. Instead of feeling sad, he had felt angry. It was too soon. Ryan wasn't ready to take over the business. He enjoyed mucking about with cars — cars had been part of his life since he was a child — but he hadn't wanted the responsibility that came with being the boss. A year later his mother had left to live in Spain, and he was completely on his own, apart from his sister and Molly.

He was brought out of his reverie when Vanessa suggested they have coffee and liqueurs in the drawing room. Ryan stayed behind in the dining room with his phone. He got through to the hospital almost immediately, probably because any patient who was able to walk had gone home for Christmas. He was told his sister was waiting for a visit from the consultant, so he couldn't speak to her at the moment, but she was doing fine and should be able to talk to him in the morning. He wished the hospital staff a happy Christmas and put his phone back in his pocket.

'How is she?' Fran asked quietly from behind him.

He hadn't heard her come into the room and she made him jump, which made her laugh.

'I'm sorry, Ryan. I didn't mean to creep up on you.'

'I'd rather it was you who made me jump than one of the ghosts of the manor. I'm sure a house like this must have some.' He smiled into those lovely amber eyes. 'And my sister is doing well, thank you. Although they never really tell you anything, do they?'

They walked back to the drawing room, where coffee was being served by Sarah. Ryan helped himself to a single-malt whisky and asked Fran what she wanted. 'You don't have to drive anywhere tonight or be at work tomorrow, so why not let your hair down a little?'

She tossed her curls like a filly shaking its head. 'I have already let my hair down, as you can see. I ask the powers that be for straight hair every night, but it never happens. Straighteners work until it rains, and then I look ridiculous, so I've given up.' She turned towards the bar. 'I think I'll have to resort to having it all cut off.'

He put his hands on her shoulders and turned her to look at him. 'Please don't.'

He could see her bewilderment. 'For goodness sake, Ryan, why should it matter to you what I do with my hair? You'll be gone in two days and never see me again.'

'That isn't going to happen, Fran, and you know it. I won't let it happen. I intend to stay around until you fall in love with me.'

He expected her to laugh, but she stared into his eyes without blinking. 'I'll have the same as you, but drop in a couple of ice cubes, please. The ice is in that insulated bucket.' She waited until her drink was in her hand. 'So you intend to hang around until I fall in love with you? You already know that's not going to happen, so you'd be wasting your time. Besides, it's a little bit conceited, don't you think?'

'Not at all. I knew I was going to marry you from the moment I first saw you. It was fate, all planned out from the start. You'll realise that in the end.' Ryan knew he had to shut up before the conversation got out of hand. He had started it off to cheer her up and make her laugh, but it had already stopped being a joke. He had just asked a woman he hardly knew to marry him, and that wasn't funny.

He watched Fran warily as she took a sip of her drink. She had a strange look in her eyes. 'You know what, Ryan Conway? You want to be careful what you wish for. A remark like that could turn around and bite you on the backside.' She patted him lightly on the cheek. 'It's lucky for you I'm not the marrying kind.'

He downed the rest of his scotch in one mouthful. He had to stop drinking, too. He had been completely sober when he told Fran he was going to marry her. What he might say if he got drunk didn't bear thinking about. He looked at his watch. Time to get Molly off to bed. She was bound to be up at the crack of dawn tomorrow, and he needed to get away from Fran before he made a complete idiot of himself.

6

Fran woke up slowly, coming out of a deep sleep. She had been dreaming, but couldn't remember what she had been dreaming about. It was dark outside, but that didn't mean it was the middle of the night. Not in December. She automatically looked for her bedside clock, and then realised it wasn't there. This was the same room she had slept in most of her life, but it still took her a minute to get her bearings.

She slid her legs out of bed and stood up, shivering in the cold. The heating had been turned down and the room was big and draughty. She had left her watch on the dressing table, which was on the other side of the room. Reaching for the bedside lamp, she knocked over the glass of water she had put there before she went to sleep, and water splashed down the front of the warm nightgown she was wearing.

Cursing softly, she turned on the small table light and swapped her wet nightgown for a dressing gown. Her watch told her it was only 4.30 a.m., and now she was wide awake with no hope of going straight back to sleep. She remembered waking in the middle of the night as a child and creeping downstairs with Lucy to make hot chocolate in the kitchen. She sighed. Those had been the fun times, when the absence of their father no longer seemed important, and tomorrow's schoolwork was their only worry.

Was there still a tub of chocolate powder in the larder? she wondered. She could almost taste the liquid on her tongue. She pushed her feet into her slippers and quietly opened her bedroom door. There was a dim light on the landing, left on by Sarah probably to stop one of the children falling down the stairs in the dark. She crept down to the hall below, wishing she could have woken Lucy like she did in the old days. An adventure was always more fun when there was someone to share it with.

She made her way to the kitchen without any trouble, but she had forgotten all about Olaf and only just managed to shut the door before he escaped into the house. His bed was in the scullery, but someone had left the door to the kitchen open and the puppy had been asleep in front of the still-warm stove. The excitement was too much for him and he promptly made a puddle on the tiled floor.

There was no way she could get cross with him. He danced around her feet, looking as if he was being wagged by his tail, rather than the other way round. She cleaned up the little puddle with kitchen roll and squatted down to stroke him. A soft footfall behind her had her leaping to her feet, and she almost lashed out without thinking before she realised Molly was the cause of her fright.

The girl gave a little scream when she

saw Fran's raised hand, and the dog immediately started dancing around and yapping. Fran had visions of the whole household waking up and appearing in the kitchen. She picked up the puppy and tucked him under one arm, putting the other arm round the scared little girl. No wonder her father used to call her a walking disaster. She pushed the thought away before it could do any damage and concentrated on restoring some sort of order to the chaos.

'It's OK, Molly,' she told the child soothingly. 'You made me jump, that's all. I'm going to make a mug of hot chocolate. I'll make you one as well, it will calm us both down.' She poked her head in the scullery and spotted a bag of dried dog food. Pouring a small amount into a saucer to keep Olaf quiet, she said, 'I couldn't sleep, so I came down to get a warm drink. Lucy and I used to do that when we were children.'

'I wish I had a sister. I couldn't sleep, either. Father Christmas hasn't been. He must think I'm still at home and he's taken my presents there instead.'

Fran remembered the old custom that had been resurrected when the boys were born. She was pretty sure Sarah would have remembered there would be an extra child in the house this year. She took Molly's hand. 'Come with me. We'll go and find out.'

Making sure Olaf was back in his bed and securely shut in, she led the way across the hall and into the dining room. Over the stone fireplace three large woollen socks hung in a row. Up until a few moments ago it hadn't entered Fran's head that Molly would need a stocking as well as the boys, but Sarah had come up trumps as always.

'You can't look in your stocking now; it has to stay there until breakfast time when George and Eric will be here as well. But Father Christmas didn't forget you, Molly. Come on, let's go back into the kitchen and get our drinks, then I'll take you back to bed.'

It only took her a few minutes to warm milk in a saucepan and whisk in some chocolate powder. Fran thought for a minute, then reached into the back of a cupboard for a tin box. Sarah kept the packet of tiny marshmallows in the same place she always had. Fran checked the sell-by date, just in case they were the ones from her childhood, but the packet was new and still within code. Molly looked surprised when Fran handed her the mug.

'What are those things on top?'

'Marshmallows. You've had them before, haven't you?'

Molly slowly shook her head, staring at the little pink and white squares floating on top of her drink. 'Not little ones like these. Only big ones in a bag.'

Fran tutted. 'You've been missing out. I shall have to take you to a café I know in London that does amazing hot chocolate. We'll have a day out and eat cupcakes with pink frosting on top.'

Molly clapped her hands. 'Yes please, Fran. I love cupcakes.'

'So do I,' a voice said from behind them. 'Can I come too?'

Molly looked scared for a minute, thinking she was going to get into trouble, but then she saw her uncle was smiling and giggled. 'No, you can't. It's a special day, just for Fran and me.'

'That's me told,' Ryan said as he came into the kitchen. 'I shall have to have a day out as well, then. A special day just for Fran and me.'

How can you feel hot all over and shiver at the same time? Fran wondered. He looked tall and imposing, even standing with bare feet in a brown checked dressing gown. She was five feet five, but she felt tiny in comparison. He was probably only just over six feet tall, but he had never looked so big before. Suddenly very conscious of her nakedness, she clutched her dressing gown more closely round her — but he noticed; she could tell by the speculative look in his eyes.

'Neither of us could sleep,' Fran said, hoping her voice didn't squeak. There was no way she was going to tell him she'd had to ditch her nightgown. 'I was making chocolate when Molly came down. Would you like some? It only takes a minute.'

'That would be nice, thank you,' he said equally politely. 'I heard you get up, Molly, but when I looked in your room you weren't there. You mustn't go wandering around the house on your own.'

'I'm sorry, Uncle Ryan,' Molly said contritely, 'but I was worried about Olaf. I thought he might be frightened of the dark, so I came down to make sure he was all right, and Fran was here.'

I'm not the only one who can lie through my teeth, Fran thought. She had turned her back to put the milk on the stove, but she almost dropped the saucepan when Ryan put a hand on her shoulder.

'I think I need to know how to make this concoction. Molly will expect her mummy to make it when we get back home.'

Fran stirred in the chocolate and

tipped the milk into a mug without spilling any. She could feel Ryan's breath on the back of her neck and for some reason this was making her hand tremble. She was adept at keeping a man at arm's length, but that was a difficult stratagem when the man in question was standing barely two inches behind you.

'The secret is the marshmallows sprinkled on top. You have to get little ones, or you can cut the big ones into little pieces, but that can get a bit messy.' She was rambling and needed to stop. 'Sit down, Ryan. You're making me nervous, hovering behind me like that.'

'Pity,' he said, taking his mug. 'I was rather enjoying it.' He moved away from her but didn't sit down. 'How are you after your fall? Any bumps or bruises?'

'No,' she said. 'My landing was surprisingly soft.' She knew she was treading on dangerous ground, but the temptation was just too much. 'How about you? I hope I didn't land on anything important.'

He grinned at her. 'Right this minute everything seems to be working just fine, but if you'd like proof . . . '

He let the sentence tail off and she laughed. She had been about to say it was about time they all went to bed, but bit the words back just in time. She didn't want to give him any more ammunition. 'I suggest you take Molly back to bed, Ryan. She's got a big day ahead of her tomorrow. I'll tidy up here and follow you in a few minutes. Olaf is quiet, so he must have gone back to sleep.'

Ryan held out his hand to Molly. 'Come on, sleepyhead.' He gave Fran a rueful grin. 'You'll have to check my injuries some other time.'

As the two of them walked towards the door, Fran went over to the window to pull the curtains closed.

'Wait!'

Ryan turned back towards her looking worried. 'What?'

Fran beckoned Molly over with a wave of her hand. 'Quickly, Molly! Come here and look out of the window.'

Molly ran over. 'Is it Father Christmas?'

Fran shook her head. 'No, it's not Father Christmas, but it's almost as good.' She pulled up a chair and Ryan lifted Molly on to it. 'Snow, Molly. Look, it's snowing on Christmas Day.'

She felt Ryan put his arm round her waist, but she didn't pull away. There was something magical about watching the snow fall outside from the cosy warmth of the kitchen. She breathed in a deep sigh of pleasure and let her head fall back against his shoulder. 'No one else knows it's snowing. Only us.'

Ryan lifted Molly down from the chair. 'Maybe tomorrow we can make a snowman.'

'We need a carrot,' Molly said, smothering a yawn. 'I made a snowman once with my daddy, and we gave him a carrot for a nose.'

'We'll find a carrot for you,' Fran

said. 'Now get off to bed, or it will be morning before you've had any sleep.'

It only took her a few minutes to tidy up the kitchen, as it wouldn't be fair to leave Sarah a mess to clean up. But she had another peep out of the window before she started upstairs. When she opened the door to her room, a frown crossed her face. A few weeks ago, snow at Christmas would have been a nuisance; something that would slow the traffic and make ugly puddles on the pavements. But now she was letting a man put his arm round her waist and sighing over a load of white stuff. Perhaps it was the fall from the treehouse. It had knocked all the sense out of her.

She had brushed her teeth to get rid of the taste of chocolate and was about to climb into bed, when someone knocked on her door. Now what? She hoped it wasn't Molly still unable to sleep. She wasn't having the child in bed with her; that would be going a step too far.

She found Ryan standing outside her door, an open bottle of champagne in one hand and two empty glasses in the other. He had that slow, sexy smile on his face. 'I still don't feel like sleep and I thought this might help, but I hate drinking alone.'

'I thought it was Molly.'

'She doesn't drink champagne. Doesn't like it.'

Fran sighed. 'Oh, for goodness sake, come inside. I'll get a bad reputation if anyone sees you standing outside my door with a champagne bottle.'

He came into her bedroom and kicked the door gently shut. 'Like in those Regency novels where a lady mustn't entertain a man in her room without a chaperone. How exciting.'

'If you think I'm going to entertain you, then you're going to be sadly disappointed. Grandmamma would not approve.'

'I can handle your grandma. She likes me.'

'She also thinks she's met you before. What's that all about?'

'I have no idea. I'm sure I've never met her.' He grinned at Fran. 'Besides, if she remembered me in my greasy overalls, she wouldn't recognise me now, would she?'

'Not if she saw you in a woolly dressing gown, no, probably not.' Fran had a vision of Ryan in greasy overalls, sweat on his brow, a spanner in his hand. To get that picture out of her head she looked down at his bare feet, but that didn't help. How could a man have sexy feet? 'You'd better go,' she said.

He took no notice. 'I found this bottle already open on my way through the dining room, and it seemed a shame to waste it. Champagne doesn't keep once it's open.'

'The bottle looks full.'

'That's exactly what I mean. It would be criminal to waste a full bottle.'

She sat down in one of the little velvet chairs by the window and watched him pour the sparkling wine into the glasses. 'Are you intending to get me drunk?'

He sat down in the other chair opposite her and handed her one of the glasses. 'I wouldn't dream of it. Besides, you've had chocolate, so you can't get drunk. Chocolate counteracts the alcoholic effect of the champagne.'

Fran frowned at him. 'You're making that up.'

'I might be, but then again it could be a scientific fact. When strawberries are served with champagne, you often find they've been dipped in chocolate first.'

'To stop people getting drunk?' She looked down at her glass and found she'd emptied it while she was talking to him. Somehow he made the rubbish coming out of his mouth sound plausible, but one glass of champagne in the early hours of the morning was quite enough.

He leant across the table and looked straight into her eyes. 'I want to know more about you, Fran. I want to know what makes you tick. For starters, what don't you like about this house? You obviously dislike being here.'

She felt tears prick at the back of her

eyes and looked away from him. 'I love this house. I've lived here most of my life, but it belongs to Annabel, my father's mother. He left us, and Annabel took us in. Lucy and I loved it here, but my mother didn't. Our father once lived here, and she had begun to hate him. She had naively believed she was a wealthy woman until he left us. Then she found out about the debts and the second mortgage — and the other woman. My father betrayed my mother and left her homeless. She had to ask her mother-in-law for help.' A tear escaped and Fran brushed it angrily away. 'She tries to pay back her debt by looking after Grandma and running the house and caring for strays.'

'Like me and Molly?'

She shook her head miserably. 'I didn't mean that. I get maudlin when I drink alcohol.'

He reached across the table and took her hand. 'I'm sorry, Fran. I'm curious by nature, and I really do want to get to know you better, but I didn't mean to upset you.'

Fran closed her eyes. She felt stupid — not a sensation she was especially fond of, particularly in front of Ryan. He now knew more about her than she had intended, and she felt exposed.

'You didn't upset me. I brought that on myself. But this works both ways. What about you, Ryan Conway? Do you have a mother and father, or any other siblings apart from your sister?'

'There's just me and my sister and Molly, I'm afraid. That's why I love your big family.' He was still holding her hand and he gave it a gentle squeeze. 'Your mother is still hurting, Fran.'

She shook her head. 'It's not hurt. It's bitterness. My father has been gone nearly twenty years and she still can't forgive him.'

'Can you?'

She slid her hand away from his. 'No, I don't think I can. Not because of what he did to me — I don't even remember him that well — but for what he did to my mother.'

'He made her stronger, and she should thank him for that. My grand-mother has been dead for some time, but she once told me every catastrophe in our lives is there for a reason. It helps to make us who we are.'

'So what makes you who you are, Ryan? Do you have some terrible trauma in your life that shaped your character?'

He just smiled at her. 'Maybe, and maybe not. It's a long and not very interesting story, so I suggest we save it for some other time. Right now we both need some sleep. It's already Christmas Day, and I have to check on Molly.' He got to his feet. 'You may not usually enjoy your time here, Fran, but I have a feeling this is going to be different.' He leant across and kissed her lightly on the lips. 'Happy Christmas.'

After he'd gone, she saw he'd left the champagne bottle on the table, so she half-filled her glass and pushed up the flowered blind over the window. Large fluffy white snowflakes were still falling, and the lawn outside was already covered. Molly was going to have her white Christmas after all.

7

The sound of voices on the landing woke Fran. It was still dark, so she carefully reached for her bedside light, avoiding the water glass, and then looked at the watch she had placed on the table. Six thirty. She clutched her head and groaned. Too much champagne last night. It was entirely her own fault, and nothing a couple of painkillers wouldn't cure; but sleeping any longer would be impossible with three children in the house, so she swung her feet out of bed and pulled on her dressing gown. The room was freezing cold, but hopefully the water would be hot. She stood outside the shower cubicle, waiting for the water to heat up before she stepped inside.

The sensation of the hot water on her bare skin was so good she stayed under the spray longer than necessary, pushing the steamed-up glass door open to reach for her towel. She almost shrieked when she saw a figure standing in front of her, until she belatedly realised it was Molly. The little girl was wearing a pink dressing gown with an appliquéd rabbit on the pocket, and pink fluffy slippers on her feet.

'What are you doing in my bedroom?' Fran said, more sharply than she intended.

The child was silent for a moment while Fran wrapped herself more securely in the towel. 'I knocked on your door but you didn't answer.' She looked Fran up and down, from her wet hair to her bare feet. 'Mummy lets me get in the shower with her.'

Fran closed her eyes and mentally counted to ten. 'I've finished my shower.' She looked round the bedroom, half-expecting Ryan to suddenly pop out of a cupboard. 'Where's your uncle?'

'He's having a bath. I want a shower, but I have to wait until he comes back because he said I'm not to get in the shower if I'm on my own.'

'So you want to use my shower?'

'Yes please.'

Fran took a fresh towel from the rack and handed it to Molly. 'Can you manage OK?'

'Yes I can, but you can come in with me if you like.'

'Thank you, but I need to dry my hair. Leave the door open and shout if you need me.' Fran had no idea at what age a child could be trusted to take a shower alone, but she presumed Molly couldn't drown in a shower cubicle. 'Make sure you wash behind your ears,' she called, before plugging in her hair dryer. She had never understood why washing behind your ears should be so important, but Sarah had always said it to her, so she was just passing it on.

She dried her hair and dressed quickly, hoping Ryan stayed in his bath long enough to give her time to put on some clothes. She had just pulled on her jeans when Molly came out of the shower wrapped in a towel.

'Can you come into my room and help me dress, please? I don't know what to wear for outside making a snowman.'

Fran sighed. She had intended putting on some lipstick, but that would have to wait for later. She felt so sorry for the poor little girl. Uncle Ryan was doing his best, but Molly needed a mother to help her with things like choosing clothes. She was only five.

The two rooms Molly and Ryan occupied were at the end of the landing next to the family bathroom. She didn't want to even think about Ryan in a bath. He wasn't only tall, he was muscular with it, so he probably had trouble fitting in a standard tub. She felt herself getting decidedly warm and tried to concentrate on something else, like Molly's meagre wardrobe.

Ryan had packed several dresses, but the only trousers Molly had were the jeans she had arrived in. Fran found a clean T-shirt and a thick cardigan to go over it, and made sure Molly put on clean underwear, including thick tights. Then she found a hanger for a pretty velvet dress she thought Molly could wear later for dinner.

She was enjoying herself plaiting Molly's long straight hair when the connecting door opened and Ryan strode into the room wearing nothing but a towel round his waist. Fran was beginning to think towels must be the dress code of the day. When he saw her he froze in mid-stride.

'Sorry. I was looking for Molly.'

Fran tried not to look at his bare chest or his bare feet. 'So here she is, all showered and dressed ready for Christmas presents and snowmen. We were just going down to breakfast.'

He backed up towards the doorway. 'I'll go and put some clothes on, then.'

'That might be a good idea,' Fran told him cheerfully. 'We don't stand on ceremony here, but we usually wear more than a towel for breakfast.'

Once he had shut the door behind him, Fran couldn't suppress a giggle.

'Your uncle did look a bit silly, didn't he, wrapped up in a towel?'

'His feet are too big.'

Not wanting to dwell on Ryan's feet, she took Molly's hand. 'Are you ready for a Christmas breakfast?'

'Do we get to look in our stockings?'

'You bet we do. If we hurry we might be the first downstairs.'

But in spite of an almost dangerous run down the big staircase, the boys had beaten them to it. George and Eric were sitting on the floor in the drawing room, small gifts spread around them. Lucy was sitting on the sofa next to Richard. She looked tired, Fran thought, but lugging that bump around all the time would be tiring. There was no sign of Vanessa or Annabel.

The twins looked up with identical grins on their faces. 'He's been,' George said. 'Father Christmas left a stocking for you, Molly.'

Fran had watched the twins attack their Christmas stockings before and she knew the drill: unhook it from the mantelpiece, tip it upside down and shake the small gifts out onto the floor. Molly treated the whole thing quite differently. She lifted her stocking carefully down and sat on the floor a little apart from George and Eric. Only then did she peep inside. Fran was dying to see what Sarah had managed to conjure up at such short notice, but she knew she couldn't hurry a process Molly was determined to enjoy however long it took.

A bag of chocolate coins came out of the sock first, then a pack of six coloured pencils and a pencil with an eraser on the end. A rolled-up colouring book was next, closely followed by a plastic ruler and a pack of butterfly stickers. Fran was beginning to think Sarah must buy in bulk in case of extra guests, which would be a sensible procedure when Vanessa might invite anyone home for the holiday. A complete pack of Girl Guides or Boy Scouts was a distinct possibility.

She frowned when she saw the small

black jewellery box Molly had now removed from the bottom of her stocking. Molly opened the box a little apprehensively. She looked up when Fran squatted down beside her, and a big smile lit up her small face.

'That's an M. That's my letter for my name.'

'Yes, it is.' Fran had never seen the necklace before. On a thin gold chain, a tiny M sparkled with what looked like real diamonds.

'Father Christmas knows my name.' The little girl's eyes were wide with wonder. 'He knows I'm Molly.'

'Of course he does,' Fran answered a trifle distractedly. 'He knows all the children's names. All the children in the whole world.'

Ryan must have put the necklace in Molly's stocking. That was the only explanation she could think of. She looked up and saw him standing in the doorway, watching Molly go through her gifts a second time. When she walked over to him, he smiled at her.

'How's the head?'

She gave him a rueful smile. 'Yours too?'

'Not too bad. Molly's having a wonderful time. Thank you again for asking us here. We would have had a miserable day on our own.'

'I'm sure you wouldn't, but I'm glad she likes it here. Did you give her the necklace? It's very pretty.'

'What necklace?'

He looked genuinely puzzled, and she realised he didn't know any more about the little pendant than she did. He would have no reason to lie about it.

'Molly got a necklace in her stocking. An M on a chain. She's thrilled to bits with it. I thought you must have given it to her.'

Ryan frowned. 'Not me. I think Sarah filled the stockings. She must have put it in there, but where she got an M from is anyone's guess.' He turned to his niece. 'Show me what you got from Father Christmas,' he said, looking at the little gifts she had laid out on the floor. 'Wow! You did well this year, didn't you?'

'I got a necklace with my letter on it. Look.' She pointed to her front, where the pendant gleamed in the light from the Christmas tree.

Ryan stood up and walked back to Fran. 'I'll have to speak to Sarah about the necklace. I don't want Molly wearing anything valuable. She might lose it.'

'It won't be valuable, Ryan, not in a stocking. Sarah just gets little things during the year for the stockings and she always has too many. That's why she made one up for Molly. The kids like the bits and bobs, even if they do only last a few days. We give out the main presents after dinner.'

He still looked uneasy, so she patted his arm. 'Stop worrying about it. Molly likes it and that's all that matters. As far as she's concerned, it came from Father Christmas.'

She walked over to a small table where an insulated coffee jug stood beside a stack of cups and saucers. She wondered why they couldn't use mugs like any normal household, but she doubted Annabel had ever seen a mug. The best china came out at each family gathering, and everyone had to sit at a table laid with silver cutlery and crystal glassware. She glanced at Ryan. He looked perfectly relaxed at the moment; but if he didn't use the right cutlery for each course at dinner, Annabel would probably throw him out on his ear. A certain amount of latitude was given to the children, but the boys already knew not to misbehave at the dinner table. Annabel could be a formidable figure when she was annoyed, and she hated bad table manners.

At that moment Sarah walked into the room carrying a serving dish filled with slices of cold ham. She was closely followed by Vanessa and Annabel. 'Everyone sit at the table,' she said, leading the way through to the dining room. 'There's bacon and eggs on the serving trolley, but it's hot, so be careful, and there are warm rolls and butter on the table. Don't eat too much,' she called to the children as they rushed to the table. 'You've got to leave room for Christmas lunch later on.'

Fran suddenly realised she was hungry. She filled her plate with ham and eggs and crispy potatoes, adding a couple of fried tomatoes for good measure. Building a snowman with the children would work off any extra calories. The snow-covered garden, visible through the French windows, looked quite beautiful, but she was glad they had managed to get here before the snowfall. Although her car seemed to handle well on dry roads, she wasn't sure how it would behave on snow and ice.

The children finished eating first after putting away enough food to keep an army going. 'Can we get down now, please?' George asked, already wriggling out of his chair.

Annabel held up her hand. 'Think about your question, George. I'm sure you *can* get down from your chair. I presume you are asking if you may.'

George sheepishly sat back in his chair. 'May I get down from the table, please, Grandma Annabel?'

She nodded her head regally, like a queen at a banquet. 'Yes you may, and so may Eric and Molly. Play with your toys quietly in the drawing room until everyone else has finished their meal.'

It amused Fran that what the children's parents thought wasn't even considered. 'Is that OK with you, Ryan?' she asked. Her grandmother was a stickler for etiquette, but appallingly rude at times, without even realising what she had done.

He smiled at her and nodded. 'Just fine with me. I can finish my breakfast in peace.'

'Molly had a necklace with her toys,' Ryan said to Sarah as she filled his cup with coffee. 'It looked more expensive than the other toys. Did you put it in her stocking?'

Sarah nodded. 'Annabel gave it to

me. She wanted it to go in Molly's stocking.'

Fran looked at her grandmother in surprise. 'I've never seen it before, Grandma. Why would you have a necklace with an M on it?'

Annabel ignored her. 'I hope you don't mind, Ryan. It belonged to my mother. She was called Martha. It's been sitting in my jewellery box for years, gathering dust because I didn't know anyone with the initial M.' She beamed at him. 'Now I do.'

Ryan kept his face expressionless. 'Are those real diamonds?'

Annabel looked genuinely puzzled for a moment. 'Of course they are, but I don't see what that has to do with anything. By the way, I've remembered why I thought I knew you.'

'Thank you for the necklace, Annabel. I'll make sure Molly takes care of it.' He smiled at her. 'I notice you said you only thought you knew me. I told you we hadn't met before.'

'But we have, although you were only

about eighteen months old at the time. You look so much like your father I thought I recognised you.'

'You knew my father?'

Fran put down her coffee cup. The whole table had gone quiet.

'What are you talking about, Annabel?' Vanessa sounded as if she thought her mother-in-law had lost her mind. 'How could you possibly know Ryan's father?'

'I knew your grandfather better,' Annabel told Ryan. 'We dated for a little while when I was about seventeen.' She sighed. 'Now they're both gone. I was so sorry to read about your father, Ryan. He was a comparatively young man when he died, wasn't he? He must only have been in his early sixties. I assume you run the business now.'

'What business?' Fran asked. The conversation had become surreal. 'I thought you were a car mechanic, Ryan.'

'I am. But when my father died

suddenly I had to take over the company.'

'Conway Cars!' Vanessa snapped her fingers. 'I should have put two and two together. The name, and Richard asking about classic cars. Your mother told me you worked in a garage, so I just assumed you were a mechanic of some kind.'

'You know what assumptions do, Mother,' Fran said.

'Yes, dear. They make an ass out of you and me.'

Ryan laughed out loud. Vanessa didn't mince her words. 'Technically my mother is right — I do work in a garage, and I like crawling about under a car getting my hands dirty.'

Fran wasn't finding any of it funny. He had led her to believe he was a garage mechanic, and now she found out he owned a business. Not one of her mother's lame ducks at all. She scowled at him. 'You'll be telling me next you're a multi-millionaire.'

'Only on paper. I don't have that sort

of money to play around with.' He grinned at her. 'No fancy yacht, I'm afraid. Just a garage and a lot of very expensive cars, none of which are actually mine.'

She nearly turned her back on him and walked out of the room, but she was afraid she might flounce and she never flounced; not intentionally, anyway. It was all her mother's fault, and her grandmother's — they attracted millionaires wherever they went, and now the lame duck had morphed into a golden goose. Fran had visualised Ryan's sister incarcerated in a crowded hospital ward, whereas in actual fact she probably had one of the best private rooms in one of the best hospitals in London.

Fran had known right from the start that Ryan would make sure his sister had the best care possible, and he was doing a good job of taking care of Molly in her mother's absence, so why was she feeling so put out? He hadn't actually lied to her about anything, but he certainly hadn't been particularly truthful. She glanced across the room. He had seated himself next to Annabel, and Vanessa had joined them. He was asking Annabel about her relationship with his grandfather and the three of them were laughing together.

Three of a kind, she thought. *Money, money, money.* Whether there was a lack of it or too much of it, money did nothing but cause problems.

Lucy called her over, and she thought again how tired her sister looked. Richard had disappeared into the drawing room to keep an eye on the children, and Lucy had moved into a more comfortable chair by the fire.

'Are you all right?' Fran asked.

Lucy nodded. 'Just a touch of backache. Sitting in the car didn't help. I might go upstairs and have a rest before the big meal in a little while. I just wanted to ask you where Mother found that gorgeous man. I thought you said he was a garage mechanic? Conway Classic Cars is known everywhere. I was reading about the company a few

134

weeks ago. They said Mr Conway had managed to track down a specific car for an Arab prince. If his father is dead, that must have been Ryan.'

Fran was still feeling put out and she still didn't know why. 'Mother led me to believe he was short of money and didn't have anywhere to go for Christmas.'

Lucy looked puzzled. 'Mother told you Ryan was short of money? Why would she do that?'

'I didn't say she told me, I said she led me to believe. As far as I'm concerned, that's the same thing.'

A slow smile spread across Lucy's face. 'You thought he was one of Mum's charity cases, didn't you? Because of her tramp last year. The poor man was only here a few hours.'

'And then I had to run him back to Horsham, where Mum originally found him,' Fran said grumpily. 'He lives in a garage near a restaurant, and if he does odd jobs for them the restaurant staff give him food and blankets. He was desperate to get away because Mum told him she could get him a proper job. He didn't want a proper job. The whole idea scared the living daylights out of man. He thought she'd kidnapped him and was going to make him her slave.'

Lucy glanced over at Ryan and sighed. 'If I wasn't in this delicate condition, I wouldn't mind making *him* my slave. Are you going to make Mum kick him out because he's here under false pretences?'

Fran laughed in spite of herself. 'I agreed to collect him and his niece because I was trying to show Mum she wasn't the only one who could help someone at Christmas. I didn't know then that Ryan was quite capable of helping himself. He could have come here in a taxi if he'd wanted to, or driven here in one of his fancy cars.'

Lucy tipped her head to one side and studied her sister thoughtfully. 'Doesn't that make you wonder why he agreed to come here with you?'

Fran shrugged. 'I have no idea.' She could feel her face getting hot. 'Like you said, he's here under false pretences.'

Lucy put her hand gently on her sister's arm. 'Not all men are like our father, Fran. There are some good ones about. Even the ones with money aren't all bad.'

Fran sighed. 'I know.' She looked out of the window, where a cold winter sun was turning the snow-covered garden into a glittering wonderland. 'I'm so glad it snowed. It makes everything perfect.'

8

Richard came back into the room with all three children. 'We're going outside to make a snowman before the snow melts. Sarah found us a carrot and an old hat and scarf. If anyone wants to join us, they're very welcome.' He looked at his wife. 'But not you, darling. You can stay in the warm and watch our efforts through the window.'

'I'm going upstairs to have a rest.' Lucy heaved herself to her feet. 'If I have a lie down now, I'll be rested for later when the children get their presents.'

'Can you manage to get upstairs on your own?' Richard asked.

Lucy nodded. 'I'm fine. Just a little too much excitement. You two behave yourselves,' she told the twins. 'Remember Molly is younger than you, and snowballs can hurt if you throw them too hard.'

Fran noticed that the children were well wrapped up. Molly was wearing borrowed rubber boots and a thick scarf, and the boys were equally well covered. She looked appealingly at Sarah. 'Do you want any help inside with the meal? I'm happy to stay if you want me to.' She really didn't want to go out in the snow; her hands would get cold and she hadn't brought her wellies with her. But Sarah was having none of it.

'I'm fine. The turkey is in the oven and the rest of the food was delivered yesterday. You go out and play with the others, Fran. It will do you good.'

How allowing herself to become freezing cold and wet could do her good, Fran had no idea. It was just a ploy to stop her sitting by the fire eating chocolates and drinking alcohol, which was what any sane person did at Christmas. She was about to protest again when Ryan appeared by her side.

'Go and put on something warm. We're going to split into two teams and make two giant snowballs, one for the head and one for the body. Richard and the twins are on one team, and you, me and Molly are on the other. We need to beat them and make the biggest snowball.' Fran opened her mouth to protest, but he pushed her towards the stairs. 'Go and get changed. I'll wait for you in the hall.'

When Fran walked into her bedroom, she found Sarah had put a quilted anorak on the bed, together with a woollen hat and scarf. Wellington boots were standing just inside the door. Fran hadn't packed for the snow. One, because it hadn't been snowing when they left, and two, because she hadn't made a snowman since she was a little girl. A memory flashed into her head and she blocked it before it could get any further. Once upon a time she had let the memories in, but even the good ones made her cry. So not anymore. There was no need to remember the past. Her new life in London was all in the present.

Grumbling to herself, she pulled on the anorak and then slid her feet into the boots. Whoever invented the full-length mirror should be should be lynched, she decided. The outfit she was wearing made her look fat and frumpy. She jammed her hair inside the woolly hat, pulled it down round her ears, and wrapped the scarf several times round her neck. Now she just looked ridiculous.

The boots were a size too big and she tripped over her own feet, nearly falling down the stairs. She scowled at Ryan when she saw him waiting at the bottom. His fleece-lined leather jacket just made him look more imposing and the black rubber boots gave him a rakish look. He looked, she thought, like a Regency stud.

'You look . . . warm,' he said.

'You don't have to be polite,' she told him churlishly. 'I already know I look ludicrous.'

He tipped his head to one side and studied her from head to toe. 'You're right, Fran, you look positively absurd, but no one will be looking at you when we get outside in the snow. We'll be having too much fun. Molly couldn't wait, so she went on ahead.'

Her mouth dropped open when he turned his back on her and headed for the door, but then her look of shock turned into a grin. She deserved that. Ryan was trying to be nice and she was being her usual boorish self. Maybe it was time to stop behaving like a spoiled child. Gritting her teeth at the thought of all that cold wet stuff out there, she followed him through the door.

Richard and the boys had already begun making their snowball. They were patting handfuls of new snow onto an already formed ball. Ryan and Molly had taken a different approach. Ryan was rolling his ball around on the ground, collecting snow as he went.

Molly was rooting around beneath a snow-covered bush as if she was searching for something, and Fran went over to find out what she was doing.

'We need sticks for his arms,' Molly told her. 'But I don't know where to look.'

'I do,' Fran said. She made her way back along the path until she found what she was looking for and then kicked at a spindly tree. 'This one loses its leaves and dies off in the winter, so it's easy to break off a few twigs.' She remembered doing the same thing years ago. 'We need a long, thin branch with bits sticking out at the end, like fingers.'

By the time they had the sticks they wanted, Ryan had a good-sized snowball ready to be used as the head of the snowman. He went over to help Richard turn the big ball into a shape that could be a body. They all helped lift the smaller ball onto the bigger one and anchor it in place.

'We don't want his head falling off,' Richard said as he made a hole for the carrot and pushed it in where he thought the snowman's nose should go.

'We need pieces of coal for eyes,' George said, jumping around with excitement. 'I'll go and get some from the coal shed.'

'I'll come with you,' Eric shouted, following his brother at a run. 'We need buttons for his front as well.'

'The idea of two young boys in a coal shed worries me a little.' Richard watched the twins disappear round a corner. 'But there's not much I can do about it.'

Fran laughed. 'If they get dirty, there's plenty of soap and hot water inside.' She looked at Molly. 'Don't you want to go with them?'

The little girl shook her head. 'I don't like getting dirty.' She shoved her hands in the pockets of her coat. 'My hands are cold.'

'So are mine,' Fran said. 'Shall we leave the men to finish the snowman and go inside to warm up?'

When Molly nodded, she tapped Ryan on the arm. 'We're going inside. Our hands are cold.'

He looked at her absently. 'OK. As long as you don't mind taking Molly with you. It won't take us long to finish up out here, then we'll be in as well.'

Fran took Molly's hand and hurried her towards the back of the house. As soon as they were out of sight, she told Molly to rub her hands together and then put them inside her coat where they would get the benefit of her body heat. Then Fran popped her head round the corner of the wall to see if the boys were back.

'We can't go inside without a snowball fight, can we? Shall we stock up on snowballs and then creep up on them?'

Molly thought it was a wonderful idea and forgot all about her cold hands, but Ryan didn't find it so funny when Fran scored a direct hit on the back of his head. Molly giggled as the snow trickled down her uncle's neck. He turned as if he'd been stung by a wasp, but by that time Fran had picked up another ball from their stash. This time she got him right over the heart and he clutched his chest dramatically, staggering around for Molly's benefit. George had already formed snow into a ball and aimed his missile at Molly. She ducked, and the snowball went over her head. By now everyone was involved, and balls of snow were flying through the air in all directions.

Fran waited until Ryan bent down to collect more snow and then pushed a handful of the cold wet stuff down the neck of his jacket. He stood up slowly and she backed away. He looked really fierce, like James Bond just before he attacks the villain. When he took a step towards her, she turned to run, but she wasn't fast enough. He caught her round the waist in a rugby tackle and brought her down in a pile of soft snow.

With a little squeal, she rolled out from under him like an eel and pushed another handful of snow in his face. She backed off again when he got to his feet, but she was unable to stifle a laugh. He had snow in his hair and stuck to his eyebrows. *Now who looks absurd?*

Molly was dancing around with glee. 'We won! We won!'

Eric ran towards Molly clutching a snowball, and Fran realised she hadn't set a very good example. But then neither had Ryan. Before Eric reached Molly, Richard grabbed the back of his son's jacket and hauled him to a stop. 'Remember Molly's a girl, Eric. You mustn't be rough with girls.'

Eric scowled. 'Fran's a girl, too.'

'Yes she is, isn't she?' Ryan said, brushing snow out of his hair. 'I don't usually have trouble remembering that, but thank you, Eric, for reminding me.'

'If you can't take the consequences, you shouldn't have started the game,' Fran told him with a grin. She looked at the snowman, who now had two black eyes and several black buttons down his front. The twiggy arms were a bit wonky, but otherwise she thought he looked great.

Richard tied the scarf in a loose knot and perched the hat on top of the snowman's head. 'A great joint effort,' he said. 'It's never been this much fun before.'

Fran was inclined to agree with that. 'Let's all go inside and warm up in the kitchen. We'll let Olaf out of the scullery so he can have a run around and work off some of his energy.'

Olaf was delighted to see them and rushed round in circles, not sure who to lick first. Sarah found a soft ball and the children took turns throwing it for him until he tired himself out.

A large bowl of hot punch stood on the kitchen table, and Sarah had put some mini-mince pies out for the children. 'Not too many,' she said sternly as they took off their wet coats and boots. 'Christmas lunch will be at two o'clock, and afterwards you can open your main presents in the grand room.'

'Can we look at our presents now?' George asked eagerly. 'So we can see how many we've got?'

'Just look at them,' Eric added for good measure.

'I'll open the door to the grand room in an hour,' Sarah told him. 'That gives you time to get warmed up and changed into dry clothes.'

The punch was made from fruit and spices and, despite being non-alcoholic, tasted absolutely delicious. Fran wasn't sure where the cockles of her heart were situated, but they were getting nicely warmed. She took her glass of punch to the oak settle that took up most of one wall of the kitchen and sat down with a little sigh of pleasure. Vanessa had padded the bench seat with a soft custom-made cushion, and Fran hoped she wasn't making it damp. She knew she had a large wet patch on the seat of her jeans. It was all Ryan's fault, but Vanessa wouldn't take kindly to indigo dye on her expensive upholstery.

Richard had gone to make sure Lucy was all right, and Ryan was sitting on the floor playing with the puppy while the children drank their punch. Fran wished she could always feel this happy. Since she had become an adult and

Lucy had left to get married, something had gone missing from the house; the elusive thing that made a house a home. Vanessa and Annabel seemed reasonably content, and Sarah was happy just looking after them both, but there had been nothing left for Fran at the manor. She had gone looking for a different life somewhere else, and she had found it in London. She had a good if slightly boring job, a place to live, and enough friends to fill her evenings. She was a modern career woman living in one of the most exciting cities in the world, and she had yet to reach her thirtieth birthday. That should be enough to make anyone happy.

The puppy had collapsed across Ryan's legs, but when Fran sat down Ryan walked into the kitchen and put Olaf back in his bed.

'You don't look happy,' he said as he came to sit beside her on the bench. 'Everyone has to be happy on Christmas Day. What's up?'

'I was reminiscing.' She turned to look at him and smiled. 'Never a good idea, particularly on Christmas Day. It was fun out there in the snow, wasn't it? I haven't had fun at Christmas for a long while. It's usually the worst time of the year for all of us, even though we all pretend we're having a great time.'

'Your father left at Christmas, didn't he?' When she nodded, he took her hand. 'It was a long time ago, Fran. Sometimes you just have to let go and get on with your life.'

'I thought I had, but coming here . . . seeing the children playing together . . . '

'Made you feel broody.'

She snatched her hand away. 'Good heavens, no! I told you I don't want children. Even if I did, I've got plenty of time. Women have children when they're a lot older than me. Look at Lucy; she's five years older than me.'

He looked at her thoughtfully. 'So it's not that you don't want children, it's just that you don't want them yet. That's sensible. We don't have to rush things. It would be nice to have some fun before we start a family. We could get married and go on a world cruise for our honeymoon, maybe. How does that sound?'

'It sounds ridiculous,' she said. She knew he was joking, but her head had filled with images of blue sea and sandy beaches. Just for a second she pictured Ryan on a beach somewhere, his bare chest tanned and gleaming in the sunshine, his smile just for her.

Richard walked into the kitchen and the image immediately dissolved, which was probably just as well. 'Lucy still has backache, but she says she's fine. She's had backache off and on all the way through this pregnancy, so I suppose I shouldn't worry. She had a warm bath and a rest, and she says the pain is a lot better now. She'll be down for lunch.'

'I'm going up to change,' Fran said. 'I might have bath as well, rather than a shower. I think I've got some bruises coming out.'

'If that's my doing, I'm sorry.' Ryan

grinned at her. 'Just let me know if you need any of those bruises kissing better.'

She managed to get out of the room before Ryan saw her blush. She had no idea what was wrong with her, blushing like a schoolgirl because some man made a suggestive remark. A few minutes later she heard the children running along the landing, then the sound of the men talking quietly as they walked past her door. She raised her arms above her head and gave a little sigh of pleasure. This is what Christmas Day should be like, she thought as she stripped off her damp clothes. A house full of family, friends and children, with plenty to eat and drink, log fires, Christmas trees and mistletoe.

She finished her bath and went back to her room, but a few minutes later she heard a knock on her bedroom door. Ryan or Molly? Still wearing nothing but her dressing gown, she opened the door a crack.

'Can I come in for a minute, Francesca?' Vanessa asked.

Fran blinked in surprise. 'Of course.' She opened the door and let her mother into the room. 'I just got out of the bath. Sit down while I dry my hair.' She couldn't imagine what had caused Vanessa to visit her in her bedroom. That was something else that hadn't happened since she was a child. 'Is something wrong, Mum?'

Vanessa shook her head. 'However I say this, Francesca, it is going to sound as if I'm interfering again — but have you got anything to wear for our Christmas lunch other than jeans?'

Fran was about to launch into a vehement protest — she would not let her mother dictate what she could and could not wear — but something stopped her. She had almost brought the jersey dress with her, but changed her mind at the last minute. Then she had worn her best trousers to dinner the night before, which left the wet denims she had just taken off.

'Sarah told me Ryan asked her if she could press the creases out of his silk shirt,' Vanessa said quietly. 'So he obviously intends to look his best.'

Fran sank down onto the bed beside her mother. 'No, I haven't got anything to wear. I was being my usual obstinate self and left my best dress behind at the flat. I now have a choice of last night's trousers or wet jeans.' She closed her eyes for a moment and then turned to look at her mother. 'Do you have any suggestions?'

'You like him, don't you?'

'I did — until I found out he owned a multi-million-pound business. I thought he was one of your lame ducks.'

'Just because he's financially solvent doesn't mean he won't need someone's help occasionally, and it gave Molly the chance to have a family Christmas. A fairy-tale Christmas with stockings over the fireplace and snow outside the windows. Don't give up on Ryan Conway just because he has money, Francesca. It wasn't money that broke up my marriage; it was lack of it.'

Fran laughed. 'Come on then, I'm

sure you didn't knock on my door just to remind me I'm not going to look my best at your special Christmas lunch. So what do you have in mind?' She couldn't think of anything her mother could suggest that would help, but she was prepared to listen.

'If you come to my room, I'll show you. I know I've put on weight over the last few years, but I never throw my favourite dresses away because I always think I'm going to get back into them one day.'

'You actually think you might have something to fit me?' Fran said doubtfully. 'I don't want to look ridiculous.'

Vanessa sighed as she got to her feet. 'Sometimes, Francesca, you have an unfortunate way with words. I can assure you I have never bought anything that would make anyone look ridiculous.'

Fran followed her mother down the landing. She didn't know what she was worried about. Looking ridiculous seemed to have become a habit since she met Ryan.

Once they were inside her room, Vanessa pulled hangers from the back of her enormous wardrobe and lay a selection of dresses on the bed. 'I can't get into any of those, so I'm sure there will be something that fits you — and won't make you look too ridiculous.'

Fran grinned at her mother. She couldn't remember the last time they had done something girly together. One of the dresses, a shift in pale lavender silk with spaghetti shoulder straps, slid on as if it was made for her. She did a twirl in front of the mirror. It was better by far than the one she had left at home, probably because it had cost several times more, but she didn't care. For once in her life she wanted to look good, and the silk shift certainly did that. It clung where it should, accentuated her good points, and slithered forgivingly over the extra few pounds on her hips. She loved it.

'I have shoes to match if you want them. The only jewellery you need are these diamond earrings I borrowed from your grandma.' Vanessa smiled when Fran raised an eyebrow. 'Once you start, you might as well go all out. It's no good doing things by half, dear; you'll spoil the effect.'

Holding the dress over her arm, the earrings clutched nervously in her hand, Fran hurried back to her own room. She wanted to get downstairs in time for a drink before the meal, something to give her a spot of Dutch courage. Although she had to dress smartly for work, the business magazine wasn't exactly in the front line where fashion was concerned. It consisted mainly of advertisements for office equipment and venues for conferences. Fran had found that several different combinations of a dark skirt and pale blouse worked just fine and saved on money.

Now she was about to swan into the grand room looking as if she actually belonged there.

9

Ryan had also spent several minutes in front of the mirror. Molly was already dressed and hopping about while she was waiting impatiently for him.

'You look very pretty, Uncle Ryan', she told him. 'Even your shoes are shiny.'

Ryan wasn't bothered about his shiny shoes. He had asked Sarah if a suit was the usual attire at the Christmas lunch, and been told that if he had one with him it would be a good idea. Strangely, he hadn't thought to pack a suit, but he had brought a dark jacket just in case, and Sarah had generously pressed his shirt and trousers. Now he felt as nervous as a kitten. He had a feeling this was his inauguration. He had to show he could present himself in a manner becoming a member of the Sutherland family, but he was between a swamp and a quagmire. Wearing a jacket to lunch might look as if he was trying to show off, particularly as Fran had told him she only wore jeans at Christmas.

Molly was still hopping from one foot to another. 'Come on, Uncle Ryan. George and Eric will be first to see the presents if we don't hurry up.'

'You've already had your mummy's present,' Ryan told her.

'But I've got yours to come,' Molly said with a smirk. 'And you always get me something really cool.'

Ryan sighed. He knew he was being ridiculous. When he personally delivered an expensive car, he had eaten in palaces and temples, so why should a medium-sized manor house give him a case of the jitters? But it wasn't the house that bothered him — that would be stupid. He was trying to impress Vanessa and Annabel — and that was even more stupid.

He took Molly by the hand. 'You look very pretty.' She was wearing the velvet dress Fran had put out for her, and he had managed to tie a ribbon in her hair. He couldn't put off the inevitable any longer. He just hoped he didn't meet Fran on the stairs and find she was still wearing her damp jeans and a sweater.

The double doors facing the staircase had been opened, and Ryan got his first glimpse of the grand room. The first thing he noticed was the tree, which was even bigger than the one in the entrance hall and filled with more decorations than the one in the dining room. This was the pièce de résistance. Topped by an antique angel, this tree had everything possible hanging from its thick green branches, including glass ornaments and crystal balls. There was hardly an inch of space that wasn't filled with something that shone or twinkled.

Once he was able to drag his eyes from the tree, Ryan turned his attention to the rest of the room. Holly covered in red berries filled large pewter urns, and on the walls trailing ivy tipped with silver hung from portraits of serious-looking ancestors. Over the doorway leading into the dining room the biggest bunch of mistletoe he had ever seen swung majestically.

He was just thinking about getting Fran under the mistletoe when Richard walked into the room with Lucy holding on to his arm. It was only then that Ryan noticed a stranger standing by the fire. The woman had her back to him, and for a moment he thought Vanessa might have invited a last-minute guest. It took him a moment, but it was the hair that gave her away. The fall of shining bronze curling on bare shoulders could only belong to Francesca Sutherland.

She turned and looked at him, and he stopped breathing. She looked every inch the lady, from her diamond earrings to her silver shoes, and he was beginning to wonder if he could actually afford her.

Molly tugged at his jacket. 'Can I

look at my presents?' she whispered, obviously as overawed by the room as he was.

'Wait until you're told it's OK,' he said absently, unable to take his eyes off Fran as she moved towards him. The dress seemed to have a life of its own, slipping and sliding over her body like ripples on a lake. For a moment he wondered if he was going to be able to speak. His throat suddenly felt dry and his collar too tight.

'You look nice,' she said. 'Where did you get the posh jacket?'

He smiled with relief. She might be wearing different clothes, but nothing else had changed. 'From the back of your car. In my job I'm never sure who I'm going to meet — a construction worker on site one day and a celebrity staying at Claridge's the next; so it pays to be ready for all eventualities.'

'So I see.' She looked him up and down. 'Mother will be pleased. She expects everyone to dress up. She'll make her entrance once everyone else is here.'

163

'You didn't mention the fact that you all dress up for lunch on Christmas Day. You could have told me when you spoke to me on the phone. Was that deliberate, or just something that slipped your mind?' He was a little bit annoyed with her. If he hadn't brought a dark jacket with him, he would have looked exactly like the charity case she wanted him to be.

She sighed. 'I suppose it was deliberate. Yes, it was deliberate, but I wasn't trying to make you look an idiot. I never dress up because I don't do what my mother tells me to do, and that's quite deliberate as well. I didn't know you had a jacket in your car, and I wanted to see if my mother would accept you as you are.' She turned her amber eyes on him. 'I was prepared to like you whatever you wore and whatever you did for a living. It honestly didn't make any difference to me. If you'd worn orange dungarees and worked in a fast-food restaurant, that would have been just fine as well.'

'I don't have my orange dungarees with me, I'm afraid. Besides, orange would have clashed with your dress.' He looked around the room. Lucy had a chair by the fire, her feet on a chintz-covered pouffe, and Molly and the twins were moving round the pile of presents beneath the tree on their hands and knees, counting on their fingers. His niece looked across the room at him and held up one hand, her fingers spread wide. She had probably got it wrong, he decided, and would be disappointed, but there was nothing he could do about that. Richard was standing by a sideboard, where a selection of bottles was grouped on a silver tray.

He held one up. 'Scotch, Ryan?'

Nodding his thanks, Ryan walked over to stand beside Fran's brother-in-law. 'How's Lucy?' He noticed Fran had pulled up a chair beside her sister and the two women were chatting together.

'Tired,' Richard said, pouring single malt into two shot glasses. 'The last few weeks are always the worst. The twins were early, but I'm hoping this one will go the course. Getting an ambulance out here in this weather could be a bit of a problem.'

Ryan realised it must have been snowing for some time. Big white flakes were drifting past the windows, and the footprints they had made earlier were nearly obliterated. A flash of red halfway down the driveway caught his eye and he moved closer to the window. What he saw made him blink in disbelief. 'Richard,' he said quietly, 'please tell me what I'm seeing is a figment of my imagination.'

Richard frowned as he peered through the glass. 'I can see your figment as well, so it must be a mass hallucination. Or then again it could be something Vanessa has organised for the children. Either way, the poor man looks as if he's having a hard time getting up the drive.'

A man dressed in a Santa suit was staggering up the drive, a sack slung over his shoulder. 'Sleigh stuck in the snow, do you think?' Ryan suggested.

'Perhaps we should open the front door. Sarah seems to have a fire going in every room, so a slide down the chimney isn't going to work.'

Richard laughed. 'We'd better find out who it is, because it's definitely not who we both think it is. But it could be anyone. An escaped convict, maybe.'

'That's not traditional prison garb, but you're right — it could be anyone.' Ryan was beginning to have serious doubts about opening the front door. He put his glass down and followed Richard out into the hallway, closing the door to the grand room behind him.

'Whoever he is,' Richard said cheerfully, 'he'll be exhausted. A walk up that long drive in snow would tax anyone. You look as if you can look after yourself, Ryan, so the two of us will be more than a match for anyone out there.'

As Richard undid the lock and turned the handle, the two men automatically moved to either side of the door. But they needn't have worried. The man in the red Father Christmas suit stumbled on the step and almost fell into the hall. The small sack slid from his back and landed beside him, spilling a couple of brightly wrapped gifts onto the polished floor. Ryan grasped one of the man's arms and Richard the other. Between them they pulled him to his feet and sat him in an upholstered chair by the door.

'Who are you?' Ryan asked.

The man's beard had come adrift, but he managed a smile through his lopsided whiskers. 'Who do you think?' When Ryan didn't answer, the man pushed his beard back into place and got to his feet. 'Where are the twins?'

Richard moved forward, looking fierce. 'What do you know about my children?'

'Ah,' the man said. 'You must be Richard. And you,' he said, looking at Ryan, 'must be Vanessa's Christmas guest. The son of a friend, I believe.' He bent down and put the little parcels back in his sack. 'I brought a small gift for Molly. Didn't want to leave anyone out.'

Before either man could answer, there was a noise behind them, and Ryan turned to see Vanessa standing completely still on the staircase. Annabel had stopped a few steps behind her.

'Jeffrey?' Vanessa appeared transfixed with shock, her voice no more than a whisper. 'What are you doing here?'

'I asked him to come,' Annabel said, her voice firm. 'This ridiculous business has gone on long enough. We need to get together and talk.'

'No!' Vanessa said sharply, turning to look at her mother-in-law. 'What on earth did you think you were doing? He can't just walk in here when he feels like it. I won't have it!'

'Be quiet, Vanessa,' Annabel said sharply. 'This is my house and I shall invite whomever I like. You invite people here every Christmas. Besides, I brought Father Christmas here for the children, not you. I won't have you spoil their pleasure.'

'Hang on a minute,' Richard said. 'Are you telling me this man is Lucy's father?' He looked at the bedraggled man in the red suit. 'You're Lucy's father?'

''Fraid so, and I need to give the children their toys as soon as possible. My boots are full of melting snow.'

Vanessa sat down on one of the steps. 'Why?' she said. 'Why did you come here, Jeffrey?'

Annabel sighed. 'Will you let him give the children their gifts, Vanessa? Just let him see them this once. The twins are his grandchildren and he's never seen them.'

'His daughters were no older than the twins when he left us. He has no business here.'

Ryan was having trouble keeping quiet, but this wasn't his problem. Not yet. If the man did anything to harm Fran, the problem would definitely become his. He was pleased when Richard took the initiative.

'This man has come a long way to

170

see his family, Vanessa. Let him give the children their presents and then you can decide what you want to do.'

Annabel moved down a step and put her hand on Vanessa's shoulder. 'Please, dear. I asked him to come here so he could see his grandchildren. Let him do that.'

Vanessa appeared to pull herself together and stood up, using the bannister rail for support. 'Very well. He can see the little ones, but then he goes back to wherever he came from.'

Ryan watched the two women with admiration. Neither would cause a scene because it would be impolite in front of their guests, so a compromise had to be reached. He looked again at the man seated in the chair. So this was Fran's father, a father she hadn't seen for nearly twenty years.

Richard looked up at the two women on the stairs. 'I won't have Lucy upset, not in her condition, so I suggest you keep your differences to yourselves. This man has come to bring the children some presents, and I suggest we let him do that. Apart from us, no one knows he isn't someone you hired to give the children a nice surprise.' He looked at Jeffrey Sutherland. 'It's doubtful Lucy or Fran will recognise him.'

The red suit should do the trick, Ryan thought. The whiskers covered most of the man's face and the suit was obviously padded. He looked like a dilapidated caricature of Santa Claus, and not a bit like a man who would inherit the manor house and the Sutherland estate when his mother died.

No one had yet decided how best to present this man to the three children, but there was no need for an elaborate plan because at that moment the door to the grand room opened and Molly stared out at them, her eyes wide. *Trust my niece to bring things to a head*, Ryan thought. Before he could speak, Molly walked forward and stood in front of Father Christmas.

'Are you the real one?' she asked.

When Sutherland nodded, her eyes moved to the sack on the floor. 'Thank you for our stockings. Did you bring us some more presents?'

The man sitting in the chair laughed through his beard and Ryan hoped it didn't fall off. At five years old, Molly still believed in everything magical, but he wasn't sure how the twins would react. They were more likely to be sceptical of the man in the damp red costume, but if gifts were involved they would probably go along with the game. Ryan fully intended keeping Fran as far away from her father as possible, and he was sure Richard would do the same with Lucy, but it would probably be best to get Jeffrey Sutherland in and out of the grand room as quickly as possible.

'Why don't you go back into the room and tell everyone who's here?' Ryan suggested.

Father Christmas got to his feet, picked up his sack, and squelched across the hall to the doorway. Molly had already rushed back inside and Ryan could hear her voice getting louder with excitement. As Jeffrey Sutherland followed her into the room, Richard started to clap, and Ryan joined in. A fanfare would have been better, he thought; but when George and Eric shouted with delight and Lucy and Fran joined in the applause, he began to think everything might work out the way Annabel had planned.

The man had a certain charisma; Ryan had to give him that. He sat in a chair with the children seated on the floor in front of him and called each in turn to receive their gift. It reminded Ryan of the cotton-wool-covered booths in department stores where a fat, bored man dished out unsuitable gifts to small, frightened children.

Once each child had a brightly wrapped box clutched in their hands, Ryan started to wonder how they were going to force the man to leave the house. The least they could do, surely, was to give him a hot drink and something to eat.

He looked across the room to where Vanessa stood apart from everyone else. Her face said it all. She wasn't going to give an inch. But while her attention was riveted on Jeffrey, Ryan was able to study her more closely. It wasn't only anger that made her stand on her own by the door; there was something else lurking beneath the surface.

Vanessa must have felt his eyes on her. She turned to look at him, and he saw what had been eluding him. Her anger was tinged with sadness, and possibly regret.

Fran came to stand beside him, and he put his worries about Vanessa out of his mind and slipped his arm round her waist.

'Who is he, Ryan? Did my mother organise it?'

'I think it was Annabel's idea,' he said evasively. 'I expect he's an out-of-work actor making a few extra pounds over the holiday. The poor man's a bit damp because he had to walk down the drive.'

He smiled down at her. 'Even Santa Claus's sleigh couldn't manage the thick snow.'

'He'll have to stay overnight. He can't be expected to drive anywhere in this weather.'

Ryan was trying desperately to think of a reply when the man in the red suit clapped his hands together to get their attention.

'The children have their gifts and I've told them they can't open them until after the Christmas meal. I believe this is a tradition, and one that must be kept. I also have small gifts for Lucinda and Francesca, but you have to remember not to open them until later.' He held out two small boxes, one in each hand. 'Please come and take them from me.'

Ryan felt as if someone had just wound him up a couple of notches too tight. Why? he wondered. Why would Jeffrey run the risk that one of his daughters might recognise him? Everything had been going fine, so why rock the boat? And then Ryan realised Jeffrey was hoping he would be recognised.

'I'll collect Lucy's gift, if you don't mind,' Richard said pleasantly. 'My wife finds it difficult to get in and out of a chair.'

Receiving a nod, Richard took the wrapped box and carried it back to his wife. Lucy accepted the gift and blew Jeffrey a kiss, something that must have delighted her father, but Fran had already slipped out of Ryan's encircling arm.

He watched as she approached the man she hadn't seen for twenty years. As far as he knew, she hadn't seen any recent photographs of him or had any contact with the man. Surely she wouldn't recognise him after all this time.

Jeffrey Sutherland took his daughter's hand. 'It's nice to meet you, Miss Sutherland. I wish you and your sister a most wonderful Christmas. I'm sorry I can't stay longer, but there is a lot for me to do at this time of the year.' He handed her a small box the same size as the one he had given Lucy. 'This may help you remember the magic of Christmas.'

He got to his feet and slowly looked round the room, taking in the decorations. 'This is beautiful; another tradition, I'm sure. I'd like to thank Richard and Ryan for rescuing me from the snow-bound driveway. Perhaps they could help me back to my transportation so I can be on my way.' He looked once more round the festive room, and then turned and walked through the doorway without looking back.

Ryan saw Annabel make a move to follow him, but she looked at Vanessa and stopped, undecided. Richard walked over and whispered something in Annabel's ear, and then he raised his hand and beckoned Ryan to follow him out into the hallway.

Once the door to the grand room was closed behind them, Ryan felt he could breathe again. He looked at Richard. 'We can't take him back outside; he'll never make it to his car. And even if he did, he'll probably have to dig the damned thing out. I don't think Father Christmas is going anywhere today.'

'I'll be fine,' Jeffrey said. He sat down and took off his boots, tipping a few drops of water onto the doormat. 'I got here all right so I'm sure I can get back again. I'm staying in that little village just down the road, so I don't have far to go.'

Both men ignored him. 'I agree,' Richard said. 'Let's get him into the kitchen where Sarah can look after him. I'm not going to be responsible for the death of Santa Claus.'

10

Fran watched the men leave the room with a frown on her face. Surely they couldn't really send that poor man out into the snow. He hadn't had time to warm up properly since he arrived. 'Why can't he stay?' she asked her mother. 'At least overnight.'

'He has somewhere else to go,' Vanessa said shortly. She put a hand to her head. 'I have a migraine, Francesca. I need a little time away from the noise of the children. I'll go into the drawing room and read quietly for an hour before lunch.'

'Reading won't help your headache,' Fran said, but her mother had already left the room.

Sarah appeared in the doorway with a large steaming bowl of mulled wine. 'Is your mother feeling ill? She walked straight past me.' Sarah put the bowl down on a heated trolley and took glass mugs from a cupboard underneath. 'I've got another one of these in the kitchen, just in case we run out.'

'My mother has a headache, or so she says. I want her to let Father Christmas stay overnight, but she's not feeling very altruistic at the moment. She wants him to leave straight away. I'm worried about him. He hasn't even had a hot drink.'

'He's fine.' Sarah poured Fran a glass of hot spiced wine and handed it to her. 'He's already had a mug of this, and I'll see he gets something to eat before he leaves. If the weather gets any worse, we'll find him a bed for the night, so you can stop worrying.' She looked across the room at the children. 'Can you make sure none of the children come into the kitchen, please, Francesca? If they see Father Christmas without his beard, it might shatter their illusions.'

'Ryan said it was Annabel's idea to invite Santa here. I agree it was a brilliant idea — the kids were thrilled to bits; but now Vanessa has disappeared and you've been left with everything to do. How can I help?'

Sarah looked round the room. Annabel was sitting with Lucy, and the children were playing with their toys. 'By keeping the children occupied. Don't worry about your mother; she gets in a state over nothing. Just keep the children out of the kitchen.'

Sarah hurried out of the room and Fran took a sip of her punch. The wine was tangy on her tongue, sweet with sugar and spices, and left a pleasant trickle of warmth on its way down. She sighed. Not only was she worried about her mother, but she was also worried about Lucy. Fran had seen her sister get up and walk around several times, obviously unable to settle comfortably. She imagined it must be really difficult to relax with seven or eight pounds of baby permanently fixed on your front.

She filled two of the glass mugs with punch and carried them over to Lucy and Annabel. If Lucy didn't drink hers, she was sure Annabel would drink it for her. 'Are you OK?' she asked her sister.

Lucy pulled a face. 'I'm having a bit of a problem with this backache. It won't go away.'

'Are you sure it's just backache?' Annabel asked. 'You could be in the early stages of labour.'

Fran fought back her feeling of panic. 'She can't be in labour.' Her voice came out as a squeak and she tried to get a hold of herself. Lucy couldn't have her baby yet; it wasn't due for another two weeks, and the weather had put paid to calling an ambulance. She had a sudden vision of everything she had imagined going wrong, and then finding there was no way to get a doctor to the house. She had never felt more helpless. 'Do you want me to get Richard?'

'I'm not in labour,' Lucy said crossly. 'I just can't get comfortable at the moment. That's perfectly normal in the last couple of weeks of pregnancy. Don't go and worry Richard; he's paranoid enough already. I'll be fine.'

'I'll keep an eye on her,' Annabel said with a smile. 'If she starts pushing, I'll let you know.'

'It's not funny, Grandma.'

Fran thought Richard should be with his wife, not sitting, drinking mulled wine with Ryan — and a fake Santa. She wandered over to the window and looked out at the snow-covered ground. The snow had stopped falling, but there was no sign of the footprints they had made earlier, and the snowman had grown in stature. His hat was now adorned with an extra inch of snow, and his twiggy arms were covered with a layer of white. There would be no traffic in or out of the manor house for quite a while.

Sarah had gone back to the kitchen, and Fran decided Richard needed to sit with Lucy. He would know better than anyone else if there was a problem. Not that they could do anything about it even if there was.

She pushed open the kitchen door and was greeted with a wave of warmth and Christmassy smells. Various pots stood on top of the stove, and the stone work surface was home to numerous foil-covered plates and dishes. The three men sat at the table, glasses of hot wine in front of them. They looked up when Fran came into the kitchen, and she couldn't work why she was getting peculiar looks from all three of them. Even Sarah seemed put out by her appearance.

'I won't get in the way, Sarah,' she said apologetically. 'I just came to get Richard. Lucy is still getting some pain with her back, and I think he needs to be with her.' Fran turned to look at her brother-in-law. 'Annabel suggested Lucy might be in labour.' She saw the look of horrified concern on his face and decided she'd better soften the blow a little. 'Lucy says she fine, just uncomfortable, and she told me that's quite normal, so I don't think you need to panic.' *Not yet, anyway,* she thought silently as Richard left the kitchen at a fast trot.

She slid onto his vacant chair and

smiled at the man who must be Santa. He looked quite different without his costume: probably somewhere in his late fifties or early sixties, his hair dark blond with white wings at the sides, and his build a lot less rotund than first appearances had suggested. He was, Fran thought, quite a good-looking man for his age.

'You look different,' she said.

He didn't reply for a moment. He looked as if he was weighing up her words and deciding on the best answer. 'Do I?'

She laughed. 'Yes, you do. I was introduced to a man in a red suit with white whiskers earlier today.'

'Ah,' he said. 'Yes, I suppose I do look a bit different.'

'Do you have a name?' she asked.

Sarah dropped a saucepan lid and cursed under her breath.

Ryan picked up an empty glass. 'Have some mulled wine, Fran. It's delicious.'

Sarah carefully put the lid back on

the saucepan and handed Fran a small mince pie. 'Have this as well; it'll keep you going until lunch. It won't be long now.'

'I've had plenty of wine already, and if I eat anything else I won't have room for lunch.' She turned back to the man without a name. 'You look familiar, as if I've met you somewhere before. Did Annabel hire you, or are you a personal friend of hers?' She definitely knew this man. The memory was there in her head, but it was a memory from a long time ago, perhaps when she was a little girl. She looked at the man again and her heart did a little flip. 'Did you know my father?'

The man sighed. 'I suppose you could say that.'

'What about the children?' Ryan interrupted. 'If Molly gets bored she'll come looking for me. We need something to keep them occupied until lunch is ready.' He snapped his fingers. 'I know. How about taking Olaf back to the grand room and letting the children

187

play with him for a bit? That should keep them busy for half an hour.' He hoped a few puppy puddles on the Persian rugs wouldn't do any lasting damage.

Fran had been worrying about leaving the children to their own devices. Richard had gone back to Lucy, so he could keep an eye on the twins, but Molly had a mind of her own. Fran took Olaf out of his bed and tucked him under her arm. Once he realised someone was paying him attention, his little tail started to wag. 'That's a great idea! I'll hand him over to Molly and then I'll be straight back. The more help you have, Sarah, the quicker lunch will be ready.' As she hurried out of the kitchen with the puppy, she heard Sarah call out that she could manage perfectly well on her own.

Molly was delighted to have her puppy to play with, and the twins came rushing over to stroke him. Fran gave strict instructions that any puddles had to be cleared up immediately. Lucy seemed more relaxed now that Richard was with her, and Fran breathed a sigh of relief. She didn't need any more excitement. She glanced into the dining room on her way back to the kitchen and saw the table had already been laid with the best cutlery. Tall glasses stood ready for the champagne, and fresh logs had been added to the fire. As Sarah had pointed out, the turkey was the only thing that had been cooked from scratch; everything else just needed heating up.

By the time she got back to the kitchen, Sarah was filling a trolley with dishes. 'Everything is ready, but perhaps you could put out some napkins, Fran, and check there are enough mats on the table to take all the hot food. Richard is going to carve the turkey, but that needs to rest for a little while.'

Fran looked at the man in the red suit. 'Why don't you come and eat with us in the dining room? I'm sure my mother won't mind.'

'It's just for family,' Ryan said quickly.

'You're not family.' Fran wished she could take her words back as soon as she said them. 'I mean, we always have visitors at Christmas. Not just family.'

'I knew what you meant,' Ryan told her. 'Now go and put napkins on the table and let Santa decide for himself what he wants to do.'

She didn't like being given orders, bus she took a pile of freshly pressed damask napkins and left the kitchen. Perhaps Santa didn't want to sit at a table full of people he didn't know. Annabel could be quite intimidating, and Vanessa was in a funny mood. Fran sighed as she distributed the napkins round the table. The day had started off so well, but now it seemed to be going downhill fast. She wanted Ryan to feel at home, but she had just told him he didn't really belong here. She was proving to be no better at diplomacy than her mother.

She started back towards the kitchen, but Richard met her halfway. He was carrying the puppy. 'Sarah is about ready to dish up, so can you see everyone to their seats, Fran? I'll put Olaf back in his bed.'

She heard the sound of the dinner gong and smiled to herself. The gong hadn't been used for some years, so she was pleased Sarah had thought his year important enough to resurrect the old tradition. The thump of small feet on the wooden floor announced the arrival of three excited children, followed by Lucy and Annabel. Richard arrived back in the room and took his place with Lucy and the twins.

Fran was just wondering if her mother had gone to sleep when Vanessa appeared in the doorway. She looked pale, and Fran wished she had been more sympathetic. The migraine must have been a real brute. Vanessa sat next to Molly and poured herself a glass of water.

'How do you feel?' Fran asked. 'Have you taken anything to help with the pain?'

'There are some things a pill won't cure,' Vanessa said tightly, and Fran wished she hadn't asked.

A few moments later Sarah came through the door pushing the trolley, followed by Ryan carrying the turkey on a silver platter. The bird was so heavy it had taken two of them to get it out of the oven, but Ryan appeared to carry it with ease. He looked amazing. He wasn't wearing a tie, but with his silk shirt open slightly at the throat he looked like the hero from a romantic novel. She hadn't met anyone for a long time that made her heart beat so fast. Like her mother said, there were some things a pill couldn't cure.

All three children said they didn't like sprouts, but when questioned they admitted they had never tried them. They just knew they wouldn't like them. The champagne had been poured and the crackers pulled, and Fran defied anyone to stay in a bad mood with three children in the house. Ryan had spoiled his romantic image with a pointed clown's hat, while Richard wore a golden crown. The children had animal masks they could wear on their heads while they ate, and the women were looking pretty in paper bonnets.

Fran knew that although Sarah supervised the food, Vanessa looked after almost everything else. The crackers had been specially chosen and the seating arrangements organised by her mother. The decorations would have been a joint effort, but Annabel always had the last word where the trimmings were concerned and her impeccable taste shone through. The table was a dream of red damask, golden place mats, and tall candles surrounded by wreaths of holly. The fire had been allowed to die down so no one would get too hot, and the children were so far particularly well-behaved.

Fran smiled at Ryan and he smiled back, and that made the day just perfect. She saw Lucy happily tucking into a large plate of food, so the backache had obviously eased up. Richard looked pretty relaxed as he helped the twins decide between mince pies and ice cream or trifle and ice cream. Neither of the boys liked Christmas pudding, but Molly thought it was wonderful when Annabel poured brandy over it and Sarah set it alight, so she decided to try the pudding with a dollop of trifle on the side.

'She'll sleep well tonight,' Vanessa said with a smile. 'There's brandy in the pudding and sherry in the trifle.'

Fran knew coffee would be served in the grand room at the same time as the formal opening of the Christmas presents. Sarah had suggested something she could give Molly, and she had carefully wrapped it before she placed it under the tree.

Once everyone had finished eating, she helped Sarah stack the trolley. The oversized dishwasher would handle the dishes, and the remains of the turkey would go in the fridge. By the time the table had been cleared the children were jumping up and down with impatience. Fran wondered if she should go and check on the stranger in the kitchen, but decided she ought to be in the grand room for the distribution of gifts. Sarah always took on the job of sorting the parcels under the tree and handing them out, and she liked everyone to be there.

Her mother had bought her a sheer silk kaftan in rainbow colours, and her grandmother's gift to her was a pair of diamond earrings, the diamonds too small to be ostentatious. Fran watched her mother open the gift she had bought for her, and smiled when she saw the pleasure on her mother's face. She had downloaded a voucher for a famous London spa, and for once her mother seemed pleased with her gift.

Vanessa came over and kissed Fran on the cheek. 'Thank you, dear. I'll make time to go to London so I can enjoy being pampered. Perhaps we could meet for lunch.'

Fran nodded doubtfully. They had tried that once before, and Vanessa had spent the whole time walking round the Underground stations giving out donations to buskers.

She took the small box tied with ribbon that Sarah had just handed to her and looked at it curiously, smiling when she saw 'Thank you, from Ryan' on the gift tag. She opened the box slowly, hoping it wasn't anything expensive. When she saw what was in the box, she smiled. Ryan had bought her a gold charm. The tiny car was a perfect replica of a Rolls Royce, even down to the distinctive RR on the front. He had also bought small gifts for Vanessa and Annabel.

She walked over to him and kissed him lightly on the lips, almost laughing out loud at his astonished expression. 'Thank you.'

'Sorry it's not the real thing.'

'If it had been, I wouldn't have accepted it, so thank you for this. I'm sorry I didn't get you anything, but I didn't know you were coming until too late.' She looked down at the charm in her hand. 'I have a gold charm bracelet my grandmother gave me, so this is a perfect gift, and it will always remind me of you.'

Goodness, she thought, as she moved away from him so he couldn't see the tears in her eyes. She was getting maudlin all of a sudden.

11

The shrieks of delight from the children had abated, and Richard had been called over to look at their presents. Ryan joined him and the two men sat of the floor, ready to make a note of who had given what to whom so the children could say a proper thank-you. Fran was about to collect up the torn wrapping paper when she realised she still had a present to open. It was the one Father Christmas had given her that morning. She had put it under the tree and forgotten all about it until Sarah found it and gave it to her.

The brightly coloured paper revealed a small flat box. *Surely not jewellery,* she thought as she removed the lid. What was inside caused a puzzled frown to crease her forehead. The tiny gold bracelet nestling in tissue paper would barely fit a small child. There was no way she would be able to get it on her wrist. For a moment she thought Santa must have got his gifts mixed up, but then she saw an engraving on the inside of the bracelet. Just one word: *Francesca*.

She turned it around in her hand. She didn't understand, and she hated mysteries. She heard her sister gasp. Of course, Lucy had been given a gift at the same time. When she looked across the room, Lucy was looking equally puzzled. Fran went over and sat beside her on the sofa.

'What was in your box, Lucy?'

Lucy held out a bracelet almost identical to Fran's. 'I remember these. They were given to us on our first birth-day, engraved with our names. I don't remember getting mine, but I remember you having yours. Mum had to push it over your chubby little fist to get it on. We had them taken off when they began to get tight. I never knew what happened to them after that.'

Fran shook her head. 'I don't

remember anything about the bracelets. Or maybe I do. I've tried so hard to forget the bad times that a lot of the good times have disappeared as well.' She looked at the little band of gold. 'I suppose it's nice to have them back, but how did our mystery Santa get hold of them?'

Lucy shook her head. 'I have no idea. Perhaps Grandma has been keeping the bracelets for us and gave them to him to pass out. I can't imagine our mother being that sentimental.'

'But why now? What's so special about this particular Christmas?'

'You brought a man to the house,' Lucy said with a grin. 'And even though you had no choice in the matter, you've never done that before. Perhaps that's what makes this Christmas special. I'm about to have a little girl, so I can have her name engraved on the bracelet alongside mine, and you look as if you've put your dislike of children on hold for the moment. Put the bracelet away, Fran, and keep it safe. You might need it one day.'

Fran decided to change the subject. For some reason, talking about Ryan and babies all in the same breath made her heart beat faster. 'Thank you for the store voucher,' she said, trying to get her thoughts back on track. 'I can use it more or less anywhere, so that's lovely. And I thought a bunch of flowers every week for three months would give you something nice to look at when you're up at two in the morning.'

Lucy laughed. 'It was a lovely idea, Fran, so thank you, but I don't intend getting up in the night. I think men should do the breastfeeding. We've already done all the really hard work.'

'Talking about that,' Fran said, 'how's your backache?'

'It niggles now and again, but I can cope with that. Ask Annabel about the bracelets. She might be able to solve our mystery.'

Fran had a better idea — go straight to the source; but Ryan caught up with her as she was about to leave the room.

He moved round in front of her, barring her way. 'Where are you off to?'

She almost told him to mind his own business. 'To the kitchen, if you don't mind,' she said shortly. She went to push past him but he caught hold of her arms.

'Look up above you, Fran. You're about to give me my Christmas present.'

She looked up, and still had her head tilted when he kissed her. Taking her completely by surprise, he managed to slip his arms round her waist and pull her in close before she had time to move away. She could feel the warmth of his body all the way down to her toes. Her brain stopped working for a few seconds, and it was only the shouts of glee from the children and Richard's slow handclap that enabled her to claim her mouth back and wriggle out of Ryan's arms.

He laughed and raised his hands in defence. 'Mistletoe,' he said. 'There's a great big bunch of it hanging over the door. I couldn't let it go to waste, could I?'

'I should have guessed you were an opportunist,' Fran said lightly. She was trying to tell herself that the kiss had just been a bit of fun and didn't really mean anything, but her still-tingling lips were telling her something completely different.

'I've always been an opportunist, Fran. I never let something I want slip between my fingers.'

'There are exceptions to every rule, Ryan,' she said, and this time she managed to slide past him.

The mystery man was on his own, slumped in his chair fast asleep with Olaf on his lap, but he opened his eyes as soon as heard her footsteps on the tiled floor. Olaf jumped down with a wag of his tail and went in search of food in the scullery.

'Hi,' Fran said. 'Are you feeling warmer now?'

He sat up in his chair and regarded her thoughtfully. 'You didn't come out here to ask me how I felt, did you, Francesca?'

She shook her head and sat down at the table. 'No. I came to ask you your name, and who you really are.'

He took a bottle of champagne out of an ice-bucket and filled two small glasses. 'If you really want to know the answers, it may take a while.'

'We're on our own for the moment, and I have plenty of time. How did you get hold of the gold bracelets?'

The man sighed. 'We're starting at the end of the story, but that's fine, as long as you promise to hear the whole of it before you pass judgement.'

Fran swallowed. She was beginning to get a nasty feeling she had just opened Pandora's box, but she nodded her agreement.

'You already know my name, Francesca. I'm Jeffrey Sutherland and I'm your father. I took the bracelets with me to remind me of everything I'd left behind. When my mother told me Lucinda was expecting a baby girl, I wanted to give her the chance to pass it on.'

'Why did you leave us?'

That was the big question; the only one that really mattered. Fran had already guessed he was her father, but she had kept telling herself it couldn't be true. Why would he come back after all this time?

'I left because I lost all our money and I didn't know how to get it back. The debts ran into millions. Vanessa knew nothing about it. She thought I could take care of you all.' He cleared his throat and blinked rapidly.

Fran could see how difficult this was for him, but she refused to show any sympathy. 'They took our house away.'

'I know. I asked my mother to let you stay with her. She had plenty of room and needed the company. She loved the idea of having you and Lucinda running around the house. It gave her a new lease on life, and she already had Sarah to help if it got too much for her.'

'Mother agreed to live with Grandma because she felt it was best for all of us.

But it wasn't just about the money, was it? How long had you been having an affair? Did you spend all our money on her?'

Jeffrey looked completely bewildered. 'What affair?'

'The other woman,' Fran said impatiently. Why was he lying? He might as well be honest about everything.

'There was no other woman. I don't know what you're talking about, Francesca. Your mother knew there would never be another woman. I adored her. I thought I would most likely go to prison if I stayed in England. I'd lost all the company's money and the shareholders were about to take me to court. They were talking about embezzlement. Mother wanted to bail me out, but it would have taken most of what Dad had left her, and I couldn't take money from anyone else. I'd already hurt too many people. I paid back as much as I could and kept just enough for a ticket to Australia, then I got lost in the crowd.'

Fran wasn't buying any of it. A

proper husband would have stayed with his wife; a proper father would have stayed with his children. Besides, there *was* another woman. Vanessa had told her so.

'So why did you come back?' she asked.

'That's a good question,' Ryan said from the doorway. 'Why did you?'

Jeffrey looked at Ryan and smiled. 'I'm glad you're here, Conway. I think you'll be good for my girl.'

'I'm not your girl,' Fran muttered.

'That's not true,' Jeffrey said. 'You'll always be my little girl. I came home this Christmas because my mother will be eighty next year and I have another grandchild on the way. I've been away long enough. It was time to come back.' He looked at Fran. 'After the little ones have gone to bed, perhaps we can all sit down and have a conversation. Speak to your mother, Francesca. She knows I've never looked at another woman, let alone had an affair. We never got divorced, so as far as I'm concerned

I'm still a married man — and I still love Vanessa as much as I did the day we got married.'

'That's rubbish! If you had loved her you would have stayed with her; been by her side when the bailiffs came knocking at the door. She would have supported you however bad it got.'

'I thought I was doing the right thing at the time, you have to believe that. I didn't want my wife visiting me in prison, or my children believing I was a criminal.'

Ryan pulled out a chair next to Fran and poured himself a glass of champagne. 'You bought a car from my father many years ago, didn't you, Jeffrey? I was only a little boy, so I don't remember what it was.'

Jeffrey smiled. 'I didn't buy a car from him; I sold him one. An AC Cobra. Money was beginning to get tight and Vanessa had just given birth to Francesca. Lucinda was five years old at that time. You can't get a couple of kids in an AC, so I sold it. Your father gave me a good price for it. It kept us going for a while.'

Olaf was back in the kitchen, fussing for food. Fran found a packet of his puppy food and poured half the contents into a bowl. She needed something to do. How could she forgive a man who had left his wife and daughters to fend for themselves? Fran was beginning to understand her mother's obsession with helping the poor. If it hadn't been for Annabel, Vanessa could have finished up out on the street.

Ryan got to his feet. 'We'd better get back. If we stay out here any longer, someone will come looking for us, and now is not the time for a long discussion.' He turned to Jeffrey. 'Will you be all right for a bit? The snow has stopped falling, but I don't think it will be gone until tomorrow, so you might as well stay the night.'

'We'll see. I need to talk to Vanessa before I leave, so I'll stay a little while longer.'

Fran walked out of the kitchen ahead

of Ryan. She was furious with him for taking over and inviting her father to stay the night. It was nothing to do with him. Her mother wanted the man out of the house, and if he froze to death that was his problem. He shouldn't have come here in the first place. She stood still and took a breath, trying to pull herself together. She needed to get away from everyone and go somewhere to clear her head.

'I'm going for a walk.'

Ryan came to a halt beside her. 'Don't be ridiculous. You're wearing a slinky dress and high heels. Where exactly do you think you're going?'

Anywhere away from you, she thought angrily. That was the trouble with men — they always thought they knew best. He had no right to tell her what to do. If she wanted to go for a walk, she would go for a walk.

'I'll go upstairs, then — if I have your permission, of course.'

'I know your father upset you, Fran, but don't take it out on me. The temperature is below freezing outside. Only a complete idiot would go for a walk in this weather.'

So she was a complete idiot, was she? Furious, she started upstairs without another word. In her room she quickly pulled on a woollen sweater and thick socks. She needed time on her own to think things through. The one thing she didn't need was Ryan's permission to leave the house. She made sure he wasn't anywhere in sight, then hurried down the stairs. Once in the hall, she grabbed her coat from the rack and pushed her feet into her rubber boots. There was still no sign of Ryan when she let herself out of the front door and headed round the back towards the secret garden.

It was a long time since she had visited the little garden, and the bushes lining the path had doubled in size. The snow covering the ground made the path difficult to see. It took her ten minutes and several abortive attempts to find the wrought-iron gate that led into the garden. Feeling a little guilty for leaving without telling Ryan, she unlatched the gate and slipped inside, closing the gate after her.

The garden had once been a little sanctuary, but now it was sadly overgrown. The recent fall of snow softened the outline of the bare bushes and turned the stone tubs and urns into miniature snowmen. The broken frame of a small greenhouse leant drunkenly against the brick wall that enclosed the garden, and a raised bed had become a sanctuary for weeds. But somewhere there was a seat under a wooden arbour. Her father had called it a place to sit and stare.

She was surprised to find the wooden structure still intact; the seat still able to take her weight in spite of a couple of missing slats, the thatched roof full of holes but keeping most of the snow from the seat. She sat down with a little sigh. The silence was complete, hushed by the blanket of snow, a place frozen in time. She watched a robin dig under a bush, completely ignoring her presence because finding his dinner was more important. Fran remembered that once Lucy had found a grass snake behind a stone, and another time they had watched a hedgehog feeding on slugs, but that had all been years ago.

It didn't take long for the cold to start seeping into her bones. She stood up, stamping her feet to get the circulation going again, apologising to the robin for disturbing him. She started back towards the gate, but this time going the opposite way round the central statue of a very cold-looking Venus. There was no path to follow, and she had only gone a few yards when her feet slipped on a patch of ice. She struggled to get her balance, panicking when she heard a cracking sound. Far too late, she remembered the ornamental pond.

The pond was only eighteen inches deep, but as she dropped feet first into the icy water she gasped with shock. She had never felt anything so cold. The water sloshed over the top of her boots, saturating her woollen socks and soaking into the bottom of her coat. She scrambled for the side of the pond, her teeth chattering, and managed to climb out. By the time she was safely back on the snow-covered paving slabs surrounding the pond, her legs and feet felt numb.

She hung on to the branch of a tree while she pulled off each boot in turn and tipped the water out. She took off her soaking socks and put the boots back on again. She couldn't get back to the house with bare feet, but if she ran as fast as she could in her boots she might be able to keep her circulation going. Thoughts of frostbite filled her head. She couldn't manage without her feet.

Her gloves were almost as wet as her socks, and she had to take them off to open the gate. Her fingers refused to work properly and she fumbled with the latch, but eventually she managed to get the gate open and start back towards the house.

She had only gone halfway when she had to stop. Her blood was starting to circulate again and the pain in her feet was excruciating. She wanted to sit down on the ground and weep, but she knew she had to keep going. Desperate not to get lost, she followed her own footsteps, her head bent, all her concentration on the imprints in the snow. When someone grabbed her from behind, she was too exhausted to make any sort of sound at all, let alone scream.

12

Ryan took the weight of her body as she sagged against him. When she turned to look at him, the sight of her pale face and blue lips scared him. He wanted to shake her. What on earth had she been thinking? He had told her not to go outside.

Belatedly, he realised that was probably the reason she *had* gone outside. With his arm round her waist, he started to hurry her along. It was almost dark and the temperature was dropping. He had his mobile phone in his pocket and thought of calling for help, but he didn't know anyone's number and he probably wouldn't be able to get a signal. The most important thing at the moment was to get her into the warm.

'What happened, Fran?' When she didn't answer he gave her a little shake. 'Are you hurt?'

'No. Just wet. I forgot the pond was there and the ice broke.' She stumbled and almost fell, leaning against him. 'My feet are going numb again.'

He felt the edge of panic. He knew he had to do something quickly, but what? By his judgement, it was about a quarter of a mile back to the house, and she wasn't going to be able to walk quickly enough. Besides that, he had read somewhere that muscular activity could make hypothermia worse. She wasn't a tiny little thing he could sweep up in his arms or carry over his shoulder. It worked OK in books and movies, but this was the real world, and Fran was wearing a thick coat soaked with water. He supposed he could get her to strip off her wet things and wrap her in *his* coat, but she'd still have bare feet.

'Undo your coat and climb on my back.'

'What?'

'Don't argue,' he said impatiently. 'Just do it.'

He helped her undo the buttons of her coat and then bent down in front of her. 'I'm going to give you a piggyback.'

This time she didn't question him. She put her arms round his neck and wrapped her legs round his waist. She seemed to weigh a ton, but he decided it was mostly the coat. He couldn't ask her to take it off, because all she had on was the stupid little dress he had admired earlier. If she had stuck to jeans and a jumper like she wanted to, it would have been a lot easier. Once he managed to stand up, he told her to kick off her boots.

'Stick your feet in the pockets of my coat and tuck your hands down the front.'

Walking was difficult in the snow, let alone running. He hoped the heat from his body was seeping through to Fran and keeping her from freezing to death. He had the back of the house in sight when the scullery door burst open and Richard ran out, closely followed by Jeffrey Sutherland. Without speaking, the two men lifted Fran from his back and carried her through the scullery into the kitchen.

Ryan stopped just inside the door, leaning forward with his hands on his knees, getting his breath back. His legs felt so weak that he wasn't sure he could manage another step. He was ashamed of himself. The macho garage owner who worked out at the sports club every week turned out to be a wimp who couldn't carry a woman a few hundred yards.

In the kitchen Sarah was rubbing each of Fran's feet in turn with a towel. 'Your feet need to come back to life gradually, but it's still going to hurt.' She looked at the men. 'I want you out of here, all of you. Right this minute Francesca needs to get out of her wet clothes.'

'What happened?' Richard asked as Ryan led the way out of the kitchen.

'She fell into the pond in the secret garden. I told her not to go outside, but she did anyway. I got worried because I couldn't find her in the house, and went looking for her. She wouldn't have made it back on her own.' He ran a hand through his hair. 'She couldn't walk, and I couldn't carry her. I felt so bloody helpless.'

Jeffrey put a hand on his shoulder. 'But you got her back safely in the end, Ryan, and that's all that matters. Thank you for saving my daughter. I shall always be in your debt for that.'

'Jeffrey didn't know Fran was missing,' Richard said. 'Lucy sent me to find her sister, and I realised you'd disappeared as well. At first I thought you were both tucked away in a bedroom somewhere, but then I noticed Fran's coat and boots had gone.'

Ryan wished with all his heart they had been tucked away in a bedroom. Next time Fran refused to listen to him, he would pick her up in his arms and head for the nearest empty room. But then reality brought him down to earth. *In your dreams*, he thought with a rueful smile. One of the things he liked most about Fran was her stubborn independence, but it had come back to bite her this time.

Vanessa got to her feet when he walked into the grand room. 'Did you find her?'

Ryan nodded. 'Sarah's looking after her. She fell into the pond in the secret garden, but she'll be all right. She just needs warming up.'

'She should be in hospital.' Vanessa looked at Annabel. 'She should be in hospital, shouldn't she, Mother?'

'Richard just tried to call an ambulance for Lucy,' Annabel said. 'All the side roads are blocked.'

Ryan looked from one woman to the other. 'What's wrong with Lucy?' He knew she was expecting a baby, but it wasn't due for weeks yet, surely.

'I think she's in the early stages of labour, but she denies it, and I suppose I could be wrong.' Annabel sighed. 'Richard tried phoning the hospital, but they said they can't get an ambulance here because the side roads are blocked and the one and only helicopter is dealing with a pile-up on the motorway. Total inefficiency, like always.'

Ryan didn't think he could deal with another crisis. He would leave Lucy to Richard and concentrate on Fran. He looked across the room at his niece. Molly was sitting on the floor playing with a doll that was dressed in baby clothes. Learning the joys of mother-hood already, he thought worriedly. 'Who bought Molly the doll?' he asked.

'It was Francesca's,' Vanessa said. 'One of her favourites when she was a child. She found it in her room and asked me to wrap it and put it under the tree.'

Molly came over to him carrying the doll. 'Can I phone Mummy and tell her what I got for Christmas, please, Uncle Ryan?'

He took his mobile phone from his pocket and looked at the signal. It was fluctuating from good to poor every few seconds.

'The signal will keep cutting out,'

Vanessa said. 'Use the house phone in the small sitting room; it'll be quiet in there.'

He took Molly's hand. 'Come on, let's go and see if we can talk to your mummy.'

★　★　★

Once the men had gone, Sarah handed Fran a large fluffy towel. 'Take everything off, Francesca. You can keep your bra and underwear on if they're completely dry, but I want you wrapped up in that towel in two minutes flat. It's important to warm you from the core out, and not the other way around. I'm going to get you a warm drink to get the process started. Can you remember exactly what happened to you?'

'Of course I can! I know hypothermia can cause confusion, Sarah, but I remember every horrible moment of it. I thought I was going to die.'

Sarah turned round from the cooker where she was warming milk. 'I think

Ryan also thought you were going to die. He was so worried about you. He's still feeling guilty for not being able to carry you all the way back in his arms like a hero.'

'What is the matter with the man? He saved my life, for goodness sake. What more does he want?'

Sarah plonked a mug of warm milk down on the table. 'I think you know the answer to that. I'm not going to spell it out for you.'

Fran took a sip of her milk. She hated warm milk. When someone knocked on the kitchen door, she pulled the big towel more closely round her. 'I only met Ryan a couple of days ago, Sarah. I don't know anything about him.'

'Of course you do. He cared enough to come looking for you and get you home safely. He's a good man, Francesca. What more do you need to know?' She opened the door and let Jeffrey back into the kitchen. 'Look after your daughter for a few minutes,' she told him. 'I'm going to get her a dressing gown and slippers, and then I'll let her mother know she's going to be OK.'

Fran was about to say she was quite well enough to get her own dressing gown, but Sarah had already gone. Now what? She didn't want to talk to her father; there was nothing to talk about. 'Where's Ryan?' she asked.

'I don't know. I didn't go into the grand room.' He gave her a half-smile. 'I didn't think I'd be welcome in there.'

'Because it's family in there,' Fran said shortly. Her father looked as if she'd slapped him, the hurt evident on his face, but forgiving wasn't that easy. 'You gave up your right to be part of our family when you left us.' She didn't want to feel sorry for him; he didn't deserve it. 'Mum had to look after us all on her own, but she's much stronger than you ever gave her credit for. We only moved here because Grandma asked us to. She said she missed her grandchildren, so Mum agreed to come and live here, but we would have managed somehow.'

Fran heard a noise behind her. When she turned around, Vanessa was standing in the doorway, a fluffy dressing gown over her arm and slippers in her hand. Ignoring Jeffrey, she went straight to her daughter.

'How are you, darling? You don't look too bad considering what happened to you. Sarah said you needed a warm robe, so I brought you mine. It may not look much, but it's cashmere so it'll feel wonderful when you get it on. She turned to her husband. 'Jeffrey, look the other way, please.'

With her father obediently turning his back, Fran unwrapped herself from the towel and slipped into the delicious warmth of her mother's robe. It even smelt of her mother's perfume, the same perfume she had worn when they were toddlers and Jeffrey had still been a part of their lives.

'Mum, stay for a minute. Lucy and I really need to know what happened and why our father left us.' She found it impossible to call Jeffrey 'Dad'. 'I think

Lucy remembers quite a lot about that time, but she won't talk to me about it.'

Jeffrey had filled a glass with champagne, which he handed to Vanessa. She took it without looking at him and sat on a chair at the table. 'Thank you.'

Fran realised this was going to be harder than she thought. If her parents weren't prepared to talk to one another, she would never get any answers. She tied the girdle of the robe more tightly round her waist and slid her feet into the slippers. She still had her milk to finish, but right now she could have done with something stronger.

'You said you didn't have an affair,' she said to Jeffrey. 'But Mum told us that was why you left.'

Jeffrey frowned. 'Why did you tell the girls that, Vanessa? You know I never thought about another woman while I was with you.'

This time Vanessa looked at him. 'What about after you left us? You're not going to tell me there weren't any other women while you were in Australia. I was stuck with two young children, so I never got the opportunity to meet anyone else even if I'd wanted to.'

'Did you *want* to meet someone else?' When she didn't answer, he smiled sadly. 'I don't suppose you'll believe me if I tell you I was too busy working to bother with women. I needed to make enough money to pay back the company's shareholders and come home to my family, and it took longer than I thought it would. Mother told me you and the girls were quite happy here. She said you didn't want to see me. I wrecked your life once, Vanessa, and I wasn't going to do it again.'

Fran looked at her mother. 'Why did you tell us he was having an affair?' It made a difference how she felt about her father. She could forgive bad judgement more easily than infidelity.

Vanessa closed her eyes for a moment. 'Because I felt stupid, I suppose. My husband left me because he didn't trust me to stand by him when he needed me. He thought I was so shallow all I cared about was his money. It was easier for me to believe there was another woman. That way I could be angry with him.' She took a gulp of her champagne and looked at Jeffrey. 'I would have done anything for you, Jeffrey. If we lost the house, so what? We still had one another — and the children. Our children. They missed you so much. Lucinda thought she must have done something to make you mad at her and that was why you left, and little Francesca kept looking for you because she thought you must be around somewhere. I kept telling them you were coming back soon, but as they got older they realised you weren't.'

Fran could see the tears running down her mother's face, but just as she was about to get to her feet her father came round the table and pulled Vanessa into his arms. She looked as if she might push him away for a moment, but then she just buried her face in his shoulder and sobbed like a child.

Fran gathered her wet clothes together and slipped silently out of the room. She met Sarah coming through the dining room with a pile of clean clothes in her arms.

'I got these out of your room so you could dress before you went upstairs.' She looked over Fran's shoulder. 'Where's your mother?'

'With my father,' Fran said. 'I think they're listening to one another at last.'

'Is it safe to leave them alone together?'

Fran took a breath. 'I hope so. They still have a lot to talk about.' She took the clothes from Sarah. 'I'll run upstairs and get changed before anyone sees me and then I'll thank Ryan properly.'

Sarah smiled. 'Try the mistletoe. That should work.'

Fran almost made it to the staircase, but Ryan appeared just as she was about to make her way up to her bedroom. 'How are you?' he said. 'You shouldn't be running around on your own. You could die of hypothermia or frostbite or something. Where's Sarah?'

'Stop it, Ryan,' she said with a smile. 'I'm perfectly fine. All I needed was warming up. I'm going upstairs now to have a hot bath and change into some dry clothes. You can stop worrying about me.'

She was about to brush past him, but he caught hold of her arm and pulled her against him. 'You'd better get it through your head that I'm never going to stop worrying about you. I'm not used to worrying that much about anybody, so it's all new to me; but as I shall keep worrying about you for the rest of my life, you might as well get used to it.'

'That's an awful lot of worrying,' she said softly, relaxing her body against his. 'Like I said, all I needed was warming up.'

She knew he was going to kiss her, and she thought she was ready for anything he could bring on, but how wrong can you be? After a few seconds she wasn't thinking at all. All his frustrated passion had condensed into that one kiss, and she knew exactly how much trouble he was having controlling himself. She desperately wanted to give in. Her bedroom was just at the top of the staircase, and she had a feeling he could carry her there quite easily, but that wasn't how she wanted it to end.

She untangled herself from his arms and put both hands on his chest, gently pushing him away. Without his support, her legs almost gave way, and she had to hold on to the bannister rail. Her lips felt bruised and her mother's robe had come undone. She was just glad no one had come into the hallway and seen them together. What had just happened would have been X-rated.

'We've both been through something very traumatic together, Ryan,' she said, trying to sound rational, 'and our bodies need some way to relieve the tension, but this isn't the right way to do it.'

He was breathing hard, his eyes slightly glazed. After a few seconds he took a deep breath and sat down on the stairs, pulling her down beside him. 'It felt right to me. You said you needed warming up and I was trying to help.'

She laughed. 'I don't know about warmed up. I think I may be slightly singed. All I wanted to do was thank you for saving my life.'

'I'll take the little episode just now as a down payment. Go up and get changed, Fran. I'll see you in the drawing room for a drink after I've put Molly to bed. The children have had quite enough for one day. Sarah made them hot chocolate and all three of them are practically asleep on their feet.'

'I'll see you later, then.' She ran past him before he could stop her again. She only had so much willpower and that had already been used up.

Once in her bedroom, she lay down on the bed and closed her eyes. Was it possible to fall in love with someone in a few days? She very much doubted it. She had read about couples during the war rushing into a hasty relationship because of the dangers all around them. And love was so unreliable, sometimes quite cruel. Fran felt she had been hurt enough already.

She was so tired, she knew if she stayed where she was she would fall asleep, so she walked to the bathroom and turned on the taps, waiting for the tub to fill. Ryan not only had money, he wanted children, and Fran had decided a long time ago that she wanted nothing to do with either. Money, or lack of it, caused nothing but problems, and children were a terrifying responsibility. Not something Fran wanted in her life.

She slipped off her mother's cashmere robe and slid into the bath. She was just fine on her own.

13

The little drawing room turned out to be a haven of tranquillity — just what Fran needed. The only other person in the room was Annabel, and she was sitting by the fire with a drink in her hand. She looked up when Fran came into the room.

'How are you, Francesca? What a dreadful thing to happen. I shall have a padlock put on the gate into the garden before someone else falls into the pond.'

'It was covered with snow, Grandma. That's why I didn't see it. It's very shallow, and I'm sure it's perfectly safe most of the time. It would be a shame to lock it away. Why don't you get a gardener to restore the secret garden? Plant some new rose bushes and maybe put some fish in the pond. The boys would like that.'

'Can you get me another Martini, dear?' Annabel held out her empty glass. 'And don't dilute it like Sarah does. She may think I'm stupid, but even at my age I still know the difference between vodka and water.' Annabel looked round the room. 'Where's your mother?'

Pouring her grandmother a drink gave Fran time to think of her reply. In the end she decided it was best to be honest. 'I don't know, Grandma. I left her in the kitchen with my father. Did you know she lied about him having an affair? He says he never looked at another woman, not even in Australia.'

Annabel gave a little shudder. 'That's where they have all those big women called Sheila, isn't it? He wouldn't be interested in them. Besides, he's always loved your mother.'

'Then why didn't you tell her Jeffrey still loves her? And why did you tell my father not to come home when he wanted to?'

Annabel reached for the glass Fran was holding out. 'Because your mother was still angry. She would have sent him away again. And you were all quite happy here with me, weren't you? I loved having you around all the time.'

Fran sighed. Annabel had been afraid they would leave if Jeffrey came home; that was why she had told him Vanessa was managing perfectly well on her own. Her two grandchildren had already left. She would have been devastated if Vanessa had gone as well. What Annabel had done had been incredibly selfish, but also understandable.

Sarah arrived next wearing a maxidress in deep mauve. 'I had to change twice,' she said. 'I helped the two men get the children to bed and got splashed with bath water.' She helped herself to a drink and came over to stand beside Fran. 'Is your mother still with Jeffrey? I haven't been back into the kitchen since I saw you. I thought it best to leave them alone.'

Fran looked towards the door. She didn't think her father would resort to violence, but she wasn't so sure about her mother. She was about to tell Sarah she'd have a look in the kitchen and make sure there weren't any bodies lying around, when Vanessa walked into the room, followed by Jeffrey.

She looked different, Fran thought, and it wasn't just her carefully disguised puffy eyes and red nose. She looked happy for the first time in years. Although that wasn't quite the right word. Vanessa Sutherland looked positively radiant. She had changed her dress, Fran noticed, and put on fresh makeup. Her eyes were extra-bright and she seemed to be smiling for no apparent reason. Fran knew that look. She had never experienced it herself, but she had seen it on the faces of her friends from time to time. She looked at her mother and frowned. A few hours ago Vanessa had hated the man who had just walked into the room behind her.

Jeffrey also looked freshly showered and shaved. He went over and kissed Annabel on the cheek. 'It's nice to be back home at last.'

Annabel smiled at her son and held out her glass. 'Another vodka martini, please, dear. Just a touch of vermouth will be fine, and get one for Vanessa.'

Fran had once asked her grandmother why she didn't drink her vodka neat instead of bothering with barely a teaspoon of vermouth, but Annabel had told her it would be uncouth. If you added vermouth and an olive, the drink became a cocktail, which was much more ladylike.

Ryan came up beside Fran as she walked over to the drinks trolley, and slid an arm round her waist. 'Don't forget we have unfinished business to take care of.' He reached for a bottle of whisky. 'Having to take a cold shower is not ideal at this time of the year.'

She filled a tall glass with white wine and soda and turned to look at him. 'Then you'd better not drink. I'd hate to see you lose your self-control.'

He just grinned at her and poured himself a shot of scotch. 'No you wouldn't. You'd love it.'

'You can be very arrogant at times, Mr Conway. Where are Lucy and Richard?'

'Still trying to get George and Eric to bed, I expect. The boys were so hyped up that Richard had to give them a good talking to. Sarah put them in the bath and they soaked her. Luckily Molly can manage a shower on her own.' He took a sip of his drink. 'Lucy still has backache, but she's making light of it.'

'I'll go and see how she is. You stay here and keep an eye on my mother and father. There is something strange going on between them and I'd hate a family scene.'

She slipped out of the room and made her way to the kitchen. There was no sign of Lucy or Richard, but Sarah was busy putting canapés on a serving dish. She refused Fran's offer of help. The table was filled with plates of cold turkey and ham and various other savoury dishes.

'Go and check on your sister,' she said. 'When you come back you can help me carry this lot into the drawing room.'

Fran could hear noises coming from the bedroom before she got to the top of the stairs. It sounded as if Lucy and Richard were arguing. She paused undecided for a minute, but when everything went quiet she knocked on the door.

Richard opened it and beckoned Fran inside. 'See if you can talk some sense into your sister, because I'm damned if I can.'

'He wants me to lie down and rest,' Lucy said crossly. 'I'm getting some niggling pains, but they're what's called Braxton-Hicks contractions. I got them last time and they lasted for days before I went into labour. He wants to call out a helicopter, which is just ridiculous. I keep telling him I'm not going to have the baby right this minute, but he won't listen. The last thing I want to do is get rushed into hospital for no reason at all.'

241

Fran didn't want to interfere in a marital dispute, but she could see her sister was getting more and more agitated, and that wasn't going to help anybody.

'How about we play it by ear, Richard? I know you're worried because the roads are still impassable, but if Lucy comes downstairs and has something to eat it will take her mind off her niggles. Are the boys settled in bed?' When he nodded, she took Lucy's hand and pulled her to her feet. 'Come on, girl. It could get quite exciting downstairs, and you don't want to miss all the fun. Our mother and father are talking again. He actually gave her a hug when she came into the kitchen, and she didn't kill him, so I'm waiting for the next instalment.'

'A hug?' Lucy looked bewildered. 'After all he did to her?'

'He never had an affair,' Fran said. 'Mum lied about that.'

'Why? I don't understand why she would do that.'

Fran shrugged. 'Neither do I, really,

but it was all so long ago it doesn't really matter. I think they still love one another.'

Lucy made a little sound of derision. 'I'll believe that when I see it.' She looked at Richard. 'Are you coming downstairs with us, or would you rather lie on the bed and sulk because I won't do what I'm told?'

He grinned at Fran. 'Thank you — I think.'

The drawing room had a different feel to it, Fran thought as she walked through the door. A warmth that had never been there before. The fire had died down to a soft glow that reflected on the Christmas tree baubles, and a few flakes of soft snow were still falling outside the window. It was a perfect Christmas scene. Her mother and father were sitting on opposite sides of the room and Vanessa seemed determined not to look at Jeffrey, but he kept looking across at her and smiling to himself. Annabel occupied her usual armchair, a straight-backed affair covered in gold brocade. Fran

243

remembered Lucy naming that chair Grandma's Throne.

She glanced over at Ryan and he smiled at her. She wished she could stop time right at that moment so everyone could stay just as they were, but she knew that wasn't possible. Time had to move on, and people and things changed every minute. All she could do right now was make sure she remembered this moment, tucking it away where she could take it out when she needed it.

Lucy sank into another armchair and Richard perched on the arm beside her. As if on cue, Sarah came in carrying the platter of canapés. 'There's more in the kitchen, but I need help carrying them in.'

Fran got to her feet. 'I said I'd help. Where are you going to put it all? On the sideboard?' When Sarah nodded, Fran headed for the door. It wasn't until she was about to go into the kitchen that she noticed Ryan behind her. She quickly picked up a serving dish loaded with tiny sandwiches. She wasn't afraid of Ryan; she was afraid of her own reaction to him. Already her heart rate had gone up a notch and her mouth was dry. Quite ridiculous, of course, and very annoying, but there didn't seem to be anything she could do about it.

'Take the plate of sausage rolls,' she said. 'We can come back for the rest.'

He just smiled, moving up behind her and putting his hands on her hips. When he started to nuzzle her neck she tried to move away, but all that did was press her body more tightly against his. Not something she had intended doing and, as it turned out, a really big mistake. He reached round and took the dish out of her hands before she dropped it. She tipped her head up to give him better access to her neck, relishing the feel of his lips on the soft spot just below her ear. She had no idea of the exact moment when he turned her around to face him, or when his lips moved from her neck to her mouth. She had never been so completely lost in raw sensation before. A regimental band could have walked through the kitchen and she wouldn't have noticed.

This time it was Ryan who stepped back. 'Not here, Fran. When I make love to you I don't want to be interrupted. I want you all to myself.'

Fran felt the heat that had already invaded everywhere else move up to her face. She had never lost control before; never wrapped herself around a man so he had to peel her off like sticky tape. She hated losing control — it made her feel embarrassed. She looked down to make sure her clothes were still where they should be and picked up her plate of sandwiches.

'We'd better get moving with the food. They'll be waiting.' And speculating, she thought. That was even more embarrassing.

She heard him laugh softly behind her, and for a moment she debated whether to throw the whole dish of sandwiches at him, but she hated wasting food.

He balanced his plate of sausage rolls

on one hand to open the door for her. 'Take a deep breath, Fran,' he whispered in her ear as she squeezed past him. 'You look a bit hot and bothered, and Sarah might wonder what we've been up to.'

As it was, Sarah insisted on going back for the last two dishes herself, so there was no need for Fran to return to the kitchen. She breathed a sigh of relief, seriously glad she wasn't going to be alone with Ryan again. She was having trouble coming to terms with the way she had behaved. What on earth had possessed her? She hadn't had that much to drink.

She glanced over at the man who was causing the problem and wondered what on earth there was about him that made her want to rip his clothes off and crawl all over him. He wasn't even classically good-looking. He was quite ordinary really, apart from his eyes, which were an indefinable shade of blue somewhere between sapphire and aquamarine. Nothing that should cause a meltdown every time he touched her.

Sarah came back into the room, not with food, but holding the hand of a very sad-looking Molly. 'I found this little one in the hallway,' she said. 'Molly was feeling sick, but we got to the washroom in time and I think she feels better now.'

'Too much tipsy trifle,' Vanessa suggested. 'Children never know when they've had enough.'

Ryan picked Molly up in his arms. 'Next time, stop eating when you feel full. It always works for me.'

Fran stroked her hand down Molly's pale face. 'But it never worked for me, not when I was your age. I always ate too much, particularly at Christmas.' She looked round the room. 'Hands up, those who've eaten too much today?'

When everyone in the room put their hands up, Molly laughed, and Ryan put her back down on her feet. 'Back to bed, young lady, because you need to get a good night's sleep. We're going home tomorrow, and you get to tell your mummy what a good time you've had. She's coming out of hospital tomorrow and you'll be able to introduce her to Olaf.'

Molly clapped her hands, her tummy problems forgotten. She waved cheerfully as she left the room with her uncle, and Fran thought how resilient children were. Whatever life threw at them, most of them turned out all right.

Quite sure she was already full, Fran was surprised to find she still had room for a few pieces of Sarah's pretty finger food. Ryan put Molly back to bed and then helped Sarah carry in the jugs of coffee. A few minutes later he came to stand beside Fran.

'Lucy looks really uncomfortable,' he said. 'Do you think she's OK?'

Fran looked worriedly at her sister. 'I have no idea. I don't know what being pregnant feels like, and I assure you I have no wish to find out. She's already had two babies, so she probably knows if she's OK or not.'

Ryan looked across the room at Lucy

and pulled a face. 'The problem being that even if she isn't OK, there's nothing we can do about it.'

'Exactly,' Fran said. She didn't want to continue this conversation. 'She's not due yet, so I'm sure everything's just fine.'

He poured himself another whisky. 'I hope you're right. Your dad didn't study midwifery while he was away, did he?'

Fran laughed. 'I doubt it. He doesn't look the type, does he?' She looked across the room at her father. 'Although he was a great dad when we were little. That's why . . . '

Ryan must have heard the catch in her voice, because he put his arm round her. 'He left you for what he thought were good reasons at the time — now he's come back to you. There's no point in regretting the past. It's already happened and you can't change it. Fate is a funny thing, Fran. I wouldn't be standing here now if my sister didn't have to stay in hospital over Christmas.'

'So are all our actions predetermined,

or do we get to choose our own fate?'

'I think we have choices;' he said cautiously. 'How about you?'

She shook her head, smiling at him. 'If I'd had a choice, no way would I have brought you here.'

It was his turn to laugh. 'I think you just walked into your own trap. If you're right, I have no control over what happens next. It will just be part of my destiny — and yours.'

She looked up at him suspiciously. 'What's going to . . . ' That was as far as she got as he pulled her close and kissed her soundly before she could protest.

'Get a room,' Richard called out with a laugh.

Ryan let her go when she kicked him on the shin. 'Sorry,' he said, 'but I had no control over that at all. It must have been written in the stars somewhere.' She went to kick him again but he moved out of the way. 'Would you like me to get you a coffee? You have a choice this time because I don't think fate really cares about your answer.'

She tilted her head to one side and frowned. 'Are you sure? Because I keep thinking of the butterfly effect. I'd hate to alter the future of the world with the wrong answer.'

Lucy struggled to her feet. 'Sorry, folks, but I can't drink coffee and I'm too full for hot chocolate, so I'm off to bed.'

Fran kissed her sister on the cheek. 'Mind how you go, big sister. Falling down the stairs would not be a good idea — and make sure you keep that little one in there for at least another day. Sarah says it's not freezing tonight, it's starting to thaw, so by tomorrow the roads should be clear enough to drive home.'

Lucy's smile looked a little strained. 'I'll do my best.'

After Lucy and Richard left the room, Vanessa moved to the sofa next to Annabel, and Jeffrey sat beside her. A nice little family scene, Fran thought, but how long it was going to last was anyone's guess. She needed a cup of coffee, but chose decaf in the hope it wouldn't keep her awake. A couple of alcoholic drinks usually sent her straight off to sleep, but her head was so full of random thoughts it was making her hyperactive. Tomorrow Ryan would drop her off at her flat and drive away with Molly. Then what? He was already talking about marriage and babies, and even if he was only joking the idea still filled her with terror.

She already had a life full of interesting people, and a job she enjoyed. To change all that because of a chance encounter seemed the height of madness. It had taken her years to break away from her mother and grandmother and find the courage to make a life of her own. Ryan wasn't the humble garage mechanic she had thought he was; instead he was the son of a multi-millionaire and the epitome of everything she despised.

She had only known him for a few days, and he was already changing her. She had dressed up for Christmas, something she had promised herself she would never do, and she had let him turn her into a quivering wreck with a couple of kisses. If fate was involved, maybe it was to prove that letting your guard down, even at Christmas, was a very big mistake.

An involuntary yawn gave her an excuse to thank everyone for their various presents and make her exit. As she crawled upstairs to her room she thought she was going to lie awake for hours, but she slid into dreamland as soon as her head touched the pillow. She would probably have stayed that way until the morning if the sound of footsteps outside her door hadn't woken her up.

14

Fran opened eyes, still blurry with sleep, and pushed herself up on her elbows. A quick look at the clock told her it was just after two o'clock in the morning. She thought immediately of Molly. Perhaps the little girl had been sick again, or maybe the sickness had been a sign of something more serious.

She climbed out of bed and pulled on her dressing gown. If it was an emergency of some sort, there was no time to worry about her hair. Once she had her feet in her slippers, she opened the door.

The first thing she noticed was that Lucy's bedroom door was open. Fran felt her heart miss a beat. If the problem wasn't Molly, it must be her sister, and for one very short moment Fran debated slipping back into her room and pretending she was still asleep.

While she was working out whether that would be so cowardly she wouldn't be able to live with herself, Sarah came out of Lucy's room. She saw Fran and held a finger to her lips. 'Shush, Francesca. We don't want to wake the children.'

Fran decided it wasn't worth pointing out to Sarah that she hadn't made a sound. She was about to ask what had happened, but Sarah beat her to it.

'Lucinda is in labour — not the very early stages, either. The silly woman didn't say anything because she was afraid Richard might call the helicopter for nothing, but now it's off somewhere rescuing people from a stranded car.'

'How are the roads?'

'Even worse than they were earlier. It started to thaw and then froze again, so now everywhere is just a sheet of ice. Richard wanted to try driving to the hospital, but I talked him out of it. Lucinda is better off here than stuck in a freezing car in the middle of nowhere.'

'So now what?'

Fran knew she wasn't helping by standing on the landing asking questions, but someone had to do something. Lucy couldn't have her baby here. There was no one who knew how to look after her.

Before Sarah could answer, Vanessa poked her head out of her bedroom door. She took one look at Fran and Sarah and then opened the door all the way. She was wearing a peach negligée that was far too thin to keep out the cold. She was about to step out onto the landing when Jeffrey appeared behind her.

Fran did a double take. Had she just seen Jeffrey in her mother's bedroom? She was about to say something when Sarah interrupted.

'Lucinda is in labour, Vanessa. The roads are frozen and the helicopter is away somewhere else.'

Jeffrey was wearing a sensible grey dressing gown with matching slippers. 'Go and put on something warm, Vannie. I'll put on some clothes and then I'll go and turn the boiler on, but it will take a while for the house to heat up.'

While her father was dressing, Fran went back into her room and pulled on her travel jeans. 'Vannie'? Fran remembered it had been her father's pet name for her mother, but since he'd left Vanessa had insisted everyone call her by her full name. She opened her door just as he was hurrying down the stairs and hoped he remembered how to get the boiler going. It usually needed a kick before it fired up.

Vanessa came back out of the bedroom in trousers and a sweater, fluffy slippers on her feet. 'If we can't get anyone to come out here, we'll have to do the best we can. Your grandmother and I have both had babies ourselves, and Jeffrey worked on a sheep farm in Australia. If he's delivered a lamb, I presume he can deliver a baby.' She frowned. 'There are a few differences, I suppose. I think you pull a lamb out feet first, and that's the last thing you want with a human baby, but everything else must be about the same.'

Fran could feel the panic rising up into her chest. In another few minutes she wasn't going to be able to breathe. 'Where's Richard?' she asked.

'He's gone to check outside. He phoned the police and the fire brigade, and they all told him the same thing — the country roads are impassable at the moment. But he won't believe it until he's seen for himself.'

Because he feels helpless, Fran thought, *and so do I.* She had never had anything to do with pregnancy. Had never seen a woman in labour, except on TV, and then she always made a point of changing channels. She was about to go into her sister's room, something she was dreading, when Ryan came up behind her and put his hands on her hips. She was getting used to the feeling of his hands on her now, so she knew who it was before she turned round.

'Lucy's in labour,' she told him before he had time to ask. 'The roads are covered in ice and the only helicopter is off somewhere else. Jeffrey has evidently delivered a sheep in Australia, so Mum seems to think that makes him a midwife. We need a doctor here, Ryan. Someone who knows what they're doing.'

He dropped a kiss on her forehead. 'Calm down, Fran. The last thing any of us can afford do is get in a panic. Fright rubs off on people. If Lucy thinks you're scared, she'll be more scared herself. She's done this before. You said she didn't have a caesarean section with the twins, so she knows what she's doing, and this time there's only one baby to worry about. Women all over the word have babies on their own every day.'

Fran managed to smile at him. If he could convince everyone that nothing was going to go wrong, he was worth his weight in gold. Apart from anything else, he had already made her feel better. Perhaps they really could get through this without it turning into a disaster. But two lives were at stake here, and everyone was behaving as if this was a normal situation.

Sarah had disappeared back into Lucy's bedroom and Fran reluctantly followed her. She had expected to see her sister rolling around in agony, but instead Lucy was sitting up in bed drinking a glass of milk.

'As long as the kids stay asleep, Fran, we'll be OK. I'll do my best not to make a noise, but if I get too loud stick a sock in my mouth. A clean one, I hasten to add.' She grinned. 'A bullet to bite on is supposed to work best, but I don't have one of those just now.' She paused, her face scrunching up in pain. 'And if I did,' she said once she could talk again, 'I might use it to shoot myself. Paracetamol doesn't work nearly as well as gas and air.'

Fran sat on the edge of the bed wishing she could take her sister's pain away. 'Is everything normal?' she asked. 'No unexpected complications or anything else to worry about?'

Lucy shook her head. 'No problems

that I know of. Even the twins did everything by the book. They arrived one after the other, just as they were supposed to, kicking and screaming for food — which they've been doing ever since.' She reached over and took Fran's hand. 'Don't be scared, little sister. You'll be doing this one day. It may hurt a bit, but it's worth all the pain in the world. Just think, in a few hours I'll be holding my baby girl.'

Her sister drew her legs up and stifled a moan as another pain hit, and Fran knew she was never going to be convinced it was all worth it. Molly was a darling, and she adored her twin nephews, but they were children. Babies, on the other hand, did nothing but sleep or cry, mostly the latter. She couldn't think of anything more frustrating than having a crying baby and not knowing what it was crying about. Perhaps when you actually became pregnant, some maternal instinct kicked in, but she couldn't imagine that happening to her. Ryan had told her he wanted babies, and that made them incompatible right from the start.

Sarah came into the room and told Fran to go down to the kitchen and make everyone a cup of tea. 'It's going to be a long night,' she said, 'so we'll probably need something to eat later on. Can you get some of the leftovers out of the freezer and thaw them out?'

Ryan was standing on the landing talking to Richard. 'I think it's starting to thaw again, but it's like a skating rink out there,' Richard said, 'with melting snow on top of ice. It would be suicide trying to drive anywhere at the moment.'

'So it looks as if it's up to us, or the women at any rate. I can't imagine I'll be much use, but you've done this before.'

'That was different. Lucy was already in hospital because she was having twins, and the room was full of people and incubators and things. This time we've got a load of amateurs who have no idea what they're doing. They're behaving as if this is all perfectly normal.'

Fran could hear the panic in his voice. 'Go in and sit with Lucy, Richard,' she said. 'And don't you dare let her see how frightened you are. Believe it or not, giving birth *is* perfectly normal. Women have babies in cars and on bathroom floors all the time. You don't actually need drugs and machines and a bevy of consultants to have a baby.' She turned to Ryan. 'You come with me. I've been told to make tea for everyone and I'll need some help.'

Looking a little shamefaced, Richard slunk back into the bedroom, and Fran headed downstairs towards the kitchen with Ryan right behind her. She needed to keep moving and only think about what she had to do next. Thinking ahead just sent her brain into a spin.

Jeffrey met them in the hallway. 'I got the boiler going. I have no idea why Annabel insists on turning it off at night. In this weather it should be left on.'

Fran grabbed the kettle and turned the tap on full, splashing herself. The man had only been in the house for a day and he was already trying to reorganise things. 'We don't want it on full-blast all night, and if we turn it down low the slightest draft blows the flame out.'

Jeffrey just grinned at her. 'In other words, mind my own business.'

Ryan walked over and took the kettle from her. 'See what food you can find, Fran. Jeffrey can help me organise the tea. If we lay everything out down here in the kitchen, when anyone wants anything they can help themselves.' He looked at Jeffrey. 'Any idea how long having a baby usually takes?'

'Not a clue,' Jeffrey said cheerfully. 'The ewes were pretty quick at the sheep station. Four hours, maybe. Sometimes you have to swing the little ones round your head to get them breathing, but I don't think that would work too well with a baby.'

Fran was beginning to feel quite ill,

what with pulling them out by their feet and swinging them round your head . . . This was her sister they were talking about, for goodness sake! She needed to think about something else entirely if she was going to stay sane. If Jeffrey was right, there wasn't going to be time to thaw the food out. She took cold ham and turkey out of the refrigerator, turned the oven on and tipped a bag of frozen rolls on to a baking tray. Ryan saw what she was doing and fetched butter and a jar of pickle from the larder. It was going to be a DIY picnic.

Jeffrey set a large teapot on the table. 'No point in carrying all the mugs and things upstairs. If anyone wants tea, they can come and get it.' He added a plastic bottle of milk and a bag of sugar.

Fran hoped her grandmother wouldn't wake up and come downstairs. Annabel always insisted on china cups and saucers for tea, and if she saw a plastic milk bottle on the table she would have a fit.

Sarah came hurrying into the kitchen. 'Sorry to leave all this to you,' she said, glancing at the table, 'but you're obviously managing just fine. Annabel woke up and I had to explain everything all over again.'

'How did she take it?' Fran asked. Her grandmother might be getting on a bit, but she was more reliable than Vanessa when it came to a crisis.

'Just said 'I told you so' and then got herself dressed. 'She's gone in to check on Lucy.'

'The water's boiled,' Jeffrey said. 'Shall we grab a cup of tea while we can?'

Fran sank down on a chair. 'Do you really think Lucy will be OK?'

'No way of telling for sure,' Sarah said, 'but Lucy's a strong woman, and birth is normally a perfectly natural process.'

'So everyone keeps saying,' Fran answered, hearing the fear in her voice and despising herself for it. 'But what if it's not?'

'Then we deal with it.' Ryan stood behind her massaging her shoulders and she felt the tension melting away. Just for a moment she wondered what she was going to do without him.

'How long did you work on the sheep farm?' she asked her father. She wasn't really interested, but she needed to talk about something that had nothing to do with what was happening upstairs.

Jeffrey handed her a mug of tea. 'We call it a sheep station in Oz, and actually I own it. I built a nice house on the land. It's got a swimming pool and plenty of bedrooms, so you can all come and stay when you want to. The little ones will love it.' He paused and looked at Sarah. 'That's one of the reasons I came back here. I want to take Vanessa back with me.'

Fran almost dropped her mug of tea. 'Back to Australia? You must be joking! Mum won't leave here.'

She felt the panic rising up inside her all over again. There was no way her mother would leave England and move to the other side of the world. She wouldn't leave her family. Fran knew she was trying to convince herself. She was the daughter who hardly ever came home, and when she did it was under protest. Vanessa was hardly likely to stay on her account.

'What about Grandma?' she asked desperately. 'What about your mother? Are you just going to abandon her again like you did before?'

Jeffrey sighed. 'I've been talking to my mother about taking Vanessa back to Australia with me. Annabel is quite happy here with Sarah. She said they might both come out for a visit while she can still get around.'

Fran felt her body stiffen with frustration and Ryan's hands tighten on her shoulders in response. She refused to believe a word her father was telling her. He was delusional. She looked at Sarah for support, and all she saw was sympathy.

'She won't go, will she, Sarah?'

'It's up to Vanessa, but I think she ought to give it a try. She hardly ever sees you, Francesca, and it's difficult for Lucy to visit very often with the children. She gets bored here. Her only interests are her charities, and she needs more than that.'

The whole thing was beyond Fran's comprehension. Jeffrey had left Vanessa. He'd walked away when she needed him the most, and now he seemed to think he could whisk her away to Australia as if nothing had happened. Fran looked up at Ryan, and he gave her shoulders a squeeze.

'Now Sarah's come back down here, let's go and check on your sister.'

Ryan kept his arm round Fran's waist until they reached the stairs and she was grateful for his support. There was a light in the hallway that was kept on all night, but the rest of the house was in darkness. Fran asked Ryan the time and he told her it was coming up to three o'clock, but she wasn't feeling tired; she was running on adrenalin and wound up like a coiled spring. She was worried sick about her sister, and now her father had turned her world upside down yet again. The one certainty in her life was the home she had been brought up in, somewhere she could always be sure of finding her mother, and now all that might change.

Richard met them at the top of the stairs. 'Vanessa keeps telling Lucy it's OK to push, but she can't have her baby here, can she? Not without any medical help. None of us knows what we're doing, do we? Not really.'

Richard was about to go to pieces, and that wasn't going to help his wife. Fran looked at Ryan and he came to the rescue.

'Go down stairs and tell Jeffrey we need him up here. He's the only one of us with any experience in birthing. While you're down there, try calling the emergency services again. Maybe the helicopter is free now and can get out here. Tell them they can land in front of the house.'

Fran hoped he was right and it would be possible to land a helicopter in the driveway. It circled an area of grass and there were no trees anywhere near. She couldn't remember if there were any overhead lines, but Vanessa or Sarah would know about that.

Annabel poked her head out of the bedroom door. She was dressed in a thick velvet robe in a plum colour, pulled in at the waist with a tasselled cord. Even with her white hair loose round her face and fur-trimmed mules on her feet, she still looked like a titled aristocrat.

'It won't be long now,' she said with a smile. 'Lucy is doing just fine, but I think Richard has reached melting point. The twins were born in hospital with lots of medical staff around and he had expected it to be the same this time. Keep him out of the way, Francesca. He's not doing any good up here.'

'Ryan sent him down to get Jeffrey.'

'Good.' Annabel smiled at Ryan. 'My son owns a sheep station or some such thing. He took a course in animal husbandry and he's used to delivering baby lambs. Lucy's baby will be about the same size as a lamb, I should think.'

Her father hadn't said anything

about animal husbandry, but Fran thought it was probably a bonus. When Jeffrey was training he probably dealt with all sorts of animals, and any little bit of extra knowledge could prove useful now.

'Lucy won't stay in bed. She's on her hands and knees on the floor,' Annabel told them.

Fran would have preferred her grandmother keep those bits of information to herself. She breathed a sigh of relief when Jeffrey appeared at the top of the stairs. 'Richard says Lucy wants to push,' she told him. 'Is that a good thing?'

Jeffrey grinned. 'That means she's cracking on nicely.' He ambled into the bedroom but came back out almost immediately. 'My eldest daughter told me in no uncertain terms that she doesn't want me anywhere near her while she's crawling around on the floor. The fact that I used to change her nappy doesn't seem to make any difference. She's doing fine, and we'll have a new baby in a little while.'

Fran watched in disbelief as he sat himself down on a chair at the top of the stairs. 'Shouldn't you be in there helping? You know about these things. We don't.'

'Not much I can do to help at the moment. If I'm needed I'll see what I can do.'

Fran heard a strange noise that was halfway between a shout and a grunt and she put her hands over her ears. Never, ever, would she go through what her sister was going through, and if she couldn't do anything helpful she might as well get out of the way. Knowing she was being a coward and hating herself for it, she turned and hurried down the stairs, another of those scary noises following her as she ran into the kitchen.

15

Ryan cursed under his breath and hurried after Fran. He wondered how long Molly would stay asleep through all the noise and excitement. He hoped the day's activities had worn her out enough to keep her out of the way a little while longer. This time, when he entered the kitchen, he heard Olaf scratching on the scullery door. He could probably keep the puppy quiet with a handful of food, but he knew that wouldn't work with Molly. She would probably tell him she'd seen *Call the Midwife* and knew exactly what to do.

Fran was standing with her back to him, leaning over the sink, and for a moment he thought she was ill, but she straightened up and turned round to give him a rueful smile.

'Don't worry, Ryan. I'm fine. I just

wish I could be more help. I hate feeling useless. I ought to be helping Lucy, like holding her hand or something, but I'm so scared I'd probably make things worse.'

He knew exactly how she felt, because he was feeling pretty useless himself. Men didn't seem to have any particular role in the birthing process. If a woman had carried his child for nine months, he'd want to be involved in the end result. He turned to Sarah. 'Is there anything we can do to help down here?'

'Make another pot of tea, Francesca,' she said. 'Ryan, you can go and find Richard. We need to calm the poor man down before he implodes. There are plenty of people looking after Lucinda already, so you'll just be in the way if you go back upstairs.' She turned towards the scullery. 'I'm going to feed the puppy before he scratches a hole in the door.'

As Ryan was about to leave the room, Jeffrey appeared in the doorway. 'We might need a couple of towels and a bowl of boiled water. It doesn't have to be hot,' he said as Ryan reached for the kettle. 'Just sterile.'

'Why?' Fran asked, and Ryan could hear the panic in her voice.

'Because we're about to have a baby,' Jeffrey told her with a grin. 'Stop worrying, baby girl. Everything is just fine.'

Ryan put an arm round Fran's waist and pulled her close, tipping her chin up so he could look into her eyes. 'Stop freaking out and make that pot of tea. Richard is probably outside trying to get a signal on his mobile phone. He's going to need a warm drink when he comes back inside.'

He dropped a quick kiss on her trembling lips and made a hasty escape. He was feeling as freaked out as Fran. He had no idea what was going on and no idea how to help. Sarah and Fran could look after the kitchen and he knew he would be no help upstairs. He checked the other downstairs rooms for Richard, but there was no sign of the man. In the end he grabbed a coat from the coat rack in the hall and pulled it on before he opened the front door.

The snow had stopped falling and there was no crackle of ice as he stepped outside. He looked up as something wet hit him on the head, and realised the icicles over the porch were dripping. It was beginning to thaw at last.

Richard was standing in the coach house talking on his phone. He finished his conversation and slipped the phone back in his pocket as Ryan approached.

'The helicopter is still tied up ferrying people to the hospital from stranded cars, but they are going to try and get an ambulance out to us. I explained the situation all over again, and the woman I spoke to said to call back if there are any problems and someone will talk us through the necessary procedure.'

Ryan wondered what the necessary procedures were, but Richard looked a lot calmer now something was being done. It had been his inability to do anything to help that had practically unhinged the poor man.

'There's fresh tea in the kitchen,' Ryan told him. 'You need something warm to drink, and a shot of whiskey in your tea might be a good idea.'

Even accounting for the atrocious condition of the roads, it shouldn't take more than half an hour for an ambulance to reach them. It wasn't as if the manor house was difficult to find, but when they went back inside the house he turned on all the outside lights. Now they were impossible to miss.

Sarah forced Richard to sit down long enough to drink a cup of tea, but as soon as he'd finished it, he went back upstairs to check on his wife.

Fran looked at her watch. 'I can't believe this is taking so long. I thought second babies came more quickly.'

Sarah smiled. 'I believe the first thing they teach a new midwife is patience. Lucy has only been in labour for about two or three hours. You can't hurry these things. Look, I tell you what you stay here with Ryan and I'll go and check on things upstairs, OK?'

When Fran nodded, Sarah grabbed a bottle of spring water from the fridge and hurried from the room. The scratching on the scullery door started up again, so Ryan made sure the door into the rest of the house was shut and let Olaf out of the scullery. The little dog was so excited he promptly made a puddle on the floor, which made Fran laugh. Ryan breathed a sigh of relief. Letting the puppy out had been the right thing to do. Fran had immediately relaxed. Once she had wiped up the puddle with kitchen roll, she picked Olaf up in her arms and cuddled him on her lap, stroking his soft fur.

'The poor little thing has been shut up for most of the day,' she said. 'We must let him have a good run tomorrow before we start for home.'

'What time do you want to leave?'

'It'll depend on Lucy, really. If they take her into hospital before she has the baby, I shall want to go and see her before we head back home.'

Ryan didn't think that was going to happen. Jeffrey had given him a look before he took off with his towels. It was a look that said things were progressing quickly and the baby would arrive very shortly. Once Sarah had left the kitchen and they were on their own, he stood behind Fran and massaged her tense shoulders again. She leant back against him, and he could feel the warmth of her body through his clothes.

'I don't want to lose you once we leave here, Fran. I want to carry on seeing you when we're back in London.' He was surprised when he felt her back stiffen. He moved away, letting his hands drop to his sides. 'Is that a problem?'

'No . . . yes . . . I don't know, Ryan.' She turned to look at him. 'There's such a lot going on right this minute that I don't know how I feel. Maybe this isn't a good time to make decisions.'

'That isn't a particularly good reason for you not to want to see me again.' He frowned at her, trying to work out what was going on in that complicated head of hers. 'Is it my money? I assure you I'm not an extravagant person. My father taught me to respect every penny.' He tried a smile, hoping to lighten the mood. 'You can pay for a couple of meals when we go out together if that makes you feel better.'

His idea of lightening the mood obviously didn't work, because she now looked as if she was about to cry.

'It has nothing to do with money, Ryan.' She waved a hand vaguely in the air. 'But I can't do this. I can't do the baby thing — not ever; and I can't let you get involved with me, if that's what you want.' A tear dribbled down her cheek and she brushed it angrily away. 'Perhaps there's something wrong with me. I must have been born without that maternal instinct that other women have. Some people really like dogs, but they don't want to have one of their own. I'm like that.'

He took her in his arms and let her

snuffle into his chest. 'I have no intention of getting you pregnant, Fran. I would very much like to have you naked in my bed, and I think about that all the time, but I promise you I haven't been thinking about starting a family. Not just yet, anyway.'

'See?' She squirmed out of his arms and glared at him. 'You said 'not just yet'. That's exactly what I mean! I don't want a baby *ever*.' He tried to hold her again but she pushed him away. 'I hate what's happening to my sister. It scares me silly, and I know I couldn't do it. There's probably a name for it, some kind of phobia. Even if I could bring myself to go through what Lucy is going through right now, I couldn't cope with the responsibility of a small child, and you need to understand all that before you say you want to carry on seeing me.'

'OK,' he said slowly. He poured tea into his mug and added milk. He was feeling quite cross with her. 'How about we forget babies for the moment? I never suggested I wanted a serious relationship right now. We've only known one another for a couple of days. I just asked if I could take you out when we get back to London. Did it occur to you that you might be assuming a bit too much after such a short time?'

Probably not quite the response she was expecting, he thought, and certainly not the best way to calm her down. The fury in her eyes was something to behold. Quite scary, in fact. He backed away in case she hit him, picking up his mug from the table. Surely she wouldn't attack him when he was holding a mug of hot tea.

'If I remember correctly, you said yesterday you intended marrying me; and, strange as it may seem, I thought that meant you were thinking about a serious relationship.' Her lip curled and she looked as if she might growl. He thought she looked magnificent. 'I was obviously mistaken, and I apologise for that; but now I don't want to go out with you for a completely different reason. I've decided I really don't like you very much.'

She took the stairs at a run, furious with him but even more furious with herself. How could she have been so stupid? She had actually thought he cared about her. Really cared about her. But it was all show, just words to get what he wanted, which was obviously to get her into bed.

She came to a halt on the landing when Sarah barred her way.

'Lucy's been doing fine, Francesca, but now there's a problem. Your father's being wonderful, but we need that ambulance.' She looked over Fran's shoulder at Ryan. 'Can you go back downstairs and wait by the front door? Get the paramedics up here as soon as they arrive. Tell them it's turned into an emergency.'

As Ryan ran back downstairs, Fran felt the floor move under her feet. For a moment everything went blurry, but she grabbed the bannister rail and managed to pull herself together. She couldn't become another patient; Lucy needed all the attention right now. 'What sort of emergency?' she whispered. 'What's gone wrong?'

'Lucy's tired. She's managed all this on a couple of paracetamol. Jeffrey thinks the baby is getting distressed. He told Lucy she has to push the baby out as quickly as possible, but I don't know how much strength she has left.'

Fran heard her father's raised voice and rushed into the bedroom. Lucy was no longer on the floor. She was lying on the bed with Jeffrey bending over her.

'Take a big breath,' he said, 'then use everything you've got. She's about ready to pop out, but she needs a bit of help from you.' He looked up at his daughter's red, sweaty face. 'You can do this, sweetheart; just one more great big push for Daddy.'

Fran heard Lucy make a noise like something from a horror movie, and Sarah ran forward holding a towel. The next minute a squalling baby was lying on her sister's chest.

Jeffrey stood up. 'Not much different to a sheep. If a lamb's having a problem, you've just got to get it out quick as you can.' He looked down at his latest grandchild and smiled. 'She's prettier than a sheep, though, that's for sure.'

Lucy couldn't stop smiling. She had obviously forgotten everything she had been through and couldn't stop gazing at her new baby girl. Richard was by her side looking just as besotted. Jeffrey was about to leave the room, but Lucy took her eyes off her baby long enough to call him back.

'Come here and give me a kiss, Daddy. I was about ready to give up. I couldn't have done this without you. Thank you so much.'

Lucy kissed Jeffrey, and then Richard shook his hand. Fran found she was so overcome with emotion that tears were running down her face again. Completely forgetting how she felt about her father, she threw her arms round his neck and gave him a hug. 'Lucy's baby might have died without you. Thank you for helping.'

He grinned. 'No worries. Go and give your new niece a cuddle.'

Fran couldn't believe what had just happened. One minute she had thought her sister was going to die, and the next Lucy was holding a little baby girl. If something had put her through all that, Fran thought, she'd probably hate it; but as she bent down over the bed the baby opened incredibly blue eyes and looked straight at her.

Still smiling, Lucy held up the towel-wrapped bundle, and Fran took her niece in her arms. She knew she couldn't possibly know what her sister was feeling, but something clutched at her heart, and she knew she would never be quite the same again.

'We're going to call her Bethany,' Lucy said, 'and we'd like you to be her godmother when we have her chris-tened.'

Fran was glad Ryan was out of the room as she felt fresh tears welling up.

288

One look from Bethany's big blue eyes had been enough to make her doubt everything she had told him.

Vanessa wanted to hold her new granddaughter, and so did Annabel. Fran hoped the baby didn't mind being passed from one person to another, but she seemed to be lapping it up. Since her first squall of protest, she had looked at each new face with interest and gurgled her appreciation.

The sound of a siren made them all turn towards the door. 'I'll go downstairs and meet the paramedics,' Sarah said. 'The little one needs to be checked over.'

Ryan popped his head through the doorway. 'The ambulance is here. How's Lucy?'

'She's fine,' Fran told him with a smile. She couldn't be angry with him while she was holding Lucy's baby. 'Meet my new niece. Her name is Bethany.'

He took the baby from her, and Fran could see how much he enjoyed holding the little bundle. He turned to Lucy.

'She's just beautiful,' he said. 'You must be very proud of yourself.'

'This is getting to be like a game of pass the parcel.' Richard held out his arms. 'Can I have my daughter back, please?'

Ryan laughed, handing the baby back to her father just as two paramedics came into the room. 'I think we should leave Lucy and Richard alone with their new daughter,' he suggested. 'How about we go downstairs and have something to eat? If Lucy and the baby are OK, we can bring a plate up for the new parents in a little while.'

Annabel said she was going back to bed for a couple of hours' sleep, but Vanessa and Jeffrey followed them downstairs to the kitchen. Fran saw the food laid out on the table and found she was suddenly incredibly hungry. They all helped themselves to cold meat and warm rolls while Sarah filled the kettle.

'We ought to be drinking champagne,' she said, 'but champagne needs to be drunk cold, and I think hot tea makes more sense in this weather.'

Jeffrey put his plate on the table and walked over to the window. 'It's thawing quite fast. Everything is dripping now. But at least I got to experience a white Christmas. I haven't seen snow in twenty years.'

Fran wanted to tell him that was entirely his fault, but she managed to keep her mouth shut. Her father might not have redeemed himself entirely — his twenty-year absence would take a lot of redeeming — but she didn't hate him anymore. Her mother had lied through her teeth to make herself look good, so they were nearly as bad as one another; the main difference being that her father had managed to escape to Australia, whereas Vanessa had been forced to remain where she was and take the consequences of her husband's actions.

Fran sighed and sat down at the table. Nothing was ever black and white. She wanted to hate Ryan, or at least dislike him intensely, but she was finding that quite hard. He sat across the table from her, tall, dark and utterly gorgeous, and she thought of the way he took care of Molly and the way he had held baby Bethany, and wished she could get to know him better. But that wasn't going to happen. Not now he knew her views on marriage and babies.

'How many sheep have you got on your farm or sheep station or whatever?' she asked. She needed idle conversation just now.

Jeffrey shrugged. 'Not a lot, compared to some. We keep to about 1,000 ewes most of the time. The staff change depending on the season.' He looked across at Fran. 'You'd make a good jillaroo if you fancy coming out to work for me.'

'That's the name for a female farm hand,' Vanessa piped up, looking pleased with herself. 'That's right, isn't it Jeffrey? Show Francesca the pictures you showed me.'

Fran had no wish to look at photos of her father's farm, but she didn't want to talk about babies, either. She was expecting him to produce a bundle of prints, but instead he took his phone out of his pocket, turned it on, and handed it to her.

'There are about fifty photos on there, but if you scroll through a few of them it will give you an idea of the size of the place.'

He was right about that, she thought. There were a lot of outbuildings, but after that she could see nothing but fields stretching all the way to the horizon. Several of them were crowded with grazing sheep, but others were green and empty. A house stood off to one side, not as big as she had expected and in no way ostentatious. It looked nice, she thought. She spotted a gleam of blue which must be the swimming pool, and thought it would be a good place for a holiday.

She passed the phone to Ryan. 'It's a big place. Much bigger than I thought.'

Ryan flipped through the photos and then handed the phone back to Jeffrey.

'You own all this?'

Jeffrey nodded. 'At the moment.' He looked at Vanessa. 'Shall we tell them what we've decided?'

She smiled at her husband. 'I'm going back to Australia with Jeffrey in a couple of weeks.'

Fran's heart sank. So she was going to lose her father again, and this time her mother as well. How selfish was that? She had begun to think they were a family again, but obviously her father had other ideas. 'I'm going to follow in Grandma's footsteps and get a couple of hours' sleep. If it keeps thawing, we should be able to get away tomorrow without any trouble.'

'Wait, Francesca.' Vanessa had taken a seat at the table beside Fran, and now she reached across to put a hand on her daughter's arm. 'I'm not staying in Australia. Neither is Jeffrey. We spent ages talking about this, and I told Jeffrey I can't leave my family and move to the other side of the world. He doesn't want to leave you girls again, either, and he wants to be near his mother.'

'So what are you going to do?' Ryan asked curiously.

'Yes, I'd like to know that as well.' Sarah put a fresh pot of tea on the table. 'Whatever you decide, it will affect all of us.'

'I'm going to sell up and move back here permanently,' Jeffrey said. 'But that will take a bit of time to complete, so Vanessa's coming with me while I sort out a buyer for the sheep station. We'll only be gone a couple of months at the most.'

At that moment a paramedic popped his head in the door. 'We're off now. Mother and baby have been checked over and they're both fine.' He grinned. 'Dad is feeling better now it's all over, as well. We'll notify the mother's local GP and he'll arrange a hospital visit when they all get back home.'

Vanessa thanked them for coming out in such dreadful weather, and told them Lucy and her family would be staying for two or three days. By then the roads should be clear enough for them to drive home. Once the paramedics had gone, she took up where Jeffrey had left off.

'As soon as he's sorted things out, Jeffrey is coming back here to manage the house for Annabel,' she said. 'He wants to get some more chickens and keep a herd of alpacas in that field of ours. He's got all sorts of plans. We might even get enough animals to have a petting farm here, and maybe take in a few visitors for the summer months.'

Fran was about to protest that Jeffrey couldn't just walk back in and take over, but then she thought why not? It would give Vanessa something positive to do, Lucy and the children would visit more often, and Annabel would have her beloved son back. Fran had no idea where she fitted into this new scenario, and once again she felt like the odd one out. Ryan was looking at her strangely, almost as if he could read her thoughts, and she felt tears pricking at the back of her eyes. She was just tired, she told herself. She needed a couple of hours' sleep before they started back to London, and then she'd be fine.

She got to her feet and gave her mother a hug. 'I'm so glad you're not leaving for good. I promise I'll visit more often if you'll have me. I know I'm not a very good daughter.'

Vanessa looked up at her with shining eyes. 'And I haven't always been a very good mother. It's going to get better, Francesca, I promise.'

'I know.' She even managed a smile for her father. 'Good night, Daddy. I'll see you again before I leave.'

Ryan moved up beside her. 'I need some sleep as well, but I need to talk to you before you go to bed.'

She yawned. Weariness had overtaken her and she wasn't sure if she was going to be able to get up the stairs. 'I'm really tired, Ryan. Can't it wait until the morning?'

He had his hand on her arm and hustled her out of the room. 'No, it can't wait. We need to sort a few things out right now.'

She wanted to tell him to stop being so bossy, but she was quite glad of his support going up the stairs. When she opened her bedroom door he followed her inside, shutting the door and pinning her against it. She told herself it was tiredness that stopped her pushing him away. She just hadn't got the strength, and when his mouth covered hers all she could do was moan. She had to put her arms round his neck to support herself, and the fact that she was kissing him back was probably the result of too much alcohol.

When she eventually broke free to take a breath, he picked her up in his arms and carried her to the bed. She felt a stab of disappointment when he laid her down gently and sat beside her. She pushed herself up on her elbows to look at him.

'What was that all about?'

He gave her a crooked smile. 'I would have thought it was fairly obvious. If it wasn't for my iron self-control, we would both be naked right now.'

She was thinking it would only take her a couple of seconds to take her clothes off, but he had said he wanted to talk.

He took a deep breath. 'You were right, I did say I wanted to marry you, and I meant every word of it. You said we need to get to know one another, and I'll go along with that, but I feel as if I've known you a lifetime already.'

He waited a moment but Fran kept quiet. He was the one who wanted to talk, so he could do the talking.

'You also said you don't ever want children, and I'll go along with that too. But I think forever is a long time and you might change your mind.' She went to speak, but he put a finger against her lips. 'I just said you *might* change your mind. Whatever you decide, I still want to marry you, because you're more important to me than having kids will ever be.'

'I'm sorry, Ryan, but that's not going to work.' When he looked as if he was about to say something else, she shook her head. 'You had your say and now it's my turn. I thought having a baby was just about pain and discomfort, and I couldn't imagine anyone willingly putting themselves through something like that. But now I know exactly why they do.' She looked up at him and saw confusion in his eyes. 'And I never thought I would meet anyone I loved enough to want to have his children. But now I have, and I don't want to miss that experience. I want to have babies with you, Ryan.'

He slid down on the bed beside her and pulled her into his arms. 'I love you, Francesca Sutherland. I hope that will do for now, because I have a terrible confession to make. I told you a lie. My iron self-control doesn't really exist. It's absolute rubbish.'

Fran lifted up her arms so he could pull her jumper over her head. 'I'm so glad you told me that,' she said. 'You had me worried there for a minute.'

They didn't get much sleep, but by the time they left for London the snow had nearly gone. Molly was sitting in the back of the car with Olaf asleep in his basket beside her, and they were all singing carols to keep themselves awake. Fran looked at Ryan, and he looked back at her and smiled.

She realised she was happier now than she had ever been in her entire life — and it was all down to fate. Or maybe just a few Christmas trees and some mistletoe.

We do hope that you have enjoyed reading this large print book.

Did you know that all of our titles are available for purchase?

We publish a wide range of high quality large print books including:
Romances, Mysteries, Classics
General Fiction
Non Fiction and Westerns

Special interest titles available in large print are:
The Little Oxford Dictionary
Music Book, Song Book
Hymn Book, Service Book

Also available from us courtesy of Oxford University Press:
Young Readers' Dictionary
(large print edition)
Young Readers' Thesaurus
(large print edition)

For further information or a free brochure, please contact us at:
Ulverscroft Large Print Books Ltd.,
The Green, Bradgate Road, Anstey,
Leicester, LE7 7FU, England.
Tel: (00 44) **0116 236 4325**
Fax: (00 44) **0116 234 0205**

A MOST UNUSUAL CHRISTMAS

Fenella J. Miller

Cressida Hadley is delighted when Lord Bromley and his family are unexpectedly obliged to spend Christmas at her family home, the Abbey. True, Bromley's brother has a broken leg, her father and the earl have taken an instant dislike to each other, and the Dowager Lady Bromley drinks too much — but Cressida is convinced she can overcome these difficulties to arrange a merry holiday season. However, she has not taken into consideration the possibility that she might fall in love with Lord Bromley himself . . .

WHERE WE BELONG

Angela Britnell

Blamed for his sister's tragic death, estranged from his family, and his career in tatters, American Broadway singing star Liam Delaroche travels to Trelanow in Cornwall, searching for a new life. Meanwhile, local school-teacher Ellie Teague is on a mission to establish her independence after jilting Will, her longtime fiancé. The attraction between the two is instant and electric. But the shadow of Liam's past looms over their growing relationship — and then the first of his bitter family members shows up in Trelanow . . .

THE WYLDES OF CHELLOW HALL

Eileen Knowles

1950s Yorkshire: Annabel journeys to her former workplace of Chellow Hall, home of the Wylde family. An unmarried mother, she has brought her baby Tommy — son and heir to one of the Wyldes — with her, feeling she should inform his father of the child's parentage. But disaster strikes when, near the Hall, she is knocked unconscious, waking later with amnesia. She has no memory whatsoever of her name, her reason for being there — or her son . . .

DISCOVERING LOVE

Wendy Kremer

When Kim, accounts manager for an archaeological excavation, meets Alex, the dig manager, a mutual attraction flourishes between them. But Alex's colleague Gloria is not so keen on Kim — might she have her eye on Alex for herself? Meanwhile, Kim's sister Julie — a brilliant mathematician, who flits from one boyfriend to another — appears to be falling in love with David, the rich sponsor of the dig. Is it a harmless flirtation, or will she end up with a broken heart?